Immigration to North America

Chinese Immigrants

Jiao Gan

Asylum Seekers

Central American Immigrants

Chinese Immigrants

Cuban Immigrants

Indian Immigrants

Mexican Immigrants

Middle Eastern Immigrants

Refugees

Rights & Responsibilities of Citizenship

South American Immigrants

Undocumented Immigration and Homeland Security

Immigration to North America

Chinese Immigrants

Jiao Gan

Senior Consulting Editor Stuart Anderson
former Associate Commissioner for Policy and Planning,
US. Citizenship and Immigration Services

Introduction by Marian L. Smith, Historian,
U.S. Citizenship and Immigration Services

Introduction by Peter A. Hammerschmidt,
former First Secretary, Permanent Mission of Canada to the United Nations

Mason Crest
450 Parkway Drive, Suite D
Broomall, PA 19008
www.masoncrest.com

©2016 by Mason Crest, an imprint of National Highlights, Inc.

All rights reserved. No part of this publication may be reproduced or transmitted in any form or by any means, electronic or mechanical, including photocopying, recording, taping, or any information storage and retrieval system, without permission from the publisher.

Printed and bound in the United States of America.

CPSIA Compliance Information: Batch #INA2016.
For further information, contact Mason Crest at 1-866-MCP-Book.

First printing
1 3 5 7 9 8 6 4 2

Library of Congress Cataloging-in-Publication Data

on file at the Library of Congress
ISBN: 978-1-4222-3684-0 (hc)
ISBN: 978-1-4222-8101-7 (ebook)

Immigration to North America series ISBN: 978-1-4222-3679-6

Table of Contents

Introduction: The Changing Face of the United States   6
    by Marian L. Smith

Introduction: The Changing Face of Canada   10
    by Peter A. Hammerschmidt

1. Beyond Gold Mountain   15
2. The Era of Revolution   21
3. Coming to America   49
4. From Chinatown to the Suburbs   61
5. Blending Traditions   75
6. Tongs and Troubles   85
7. Part of the Mosaic, Part of the Melting Pot   97

Famous Chinese Americans   102
Series Glossary of Key Terms   104
Further Reading   105
Internet Resources   106
Index   107
Contributors   111

KEY ICONS TO LOOK FOR:

Words to Understand: These words with their easy-to-understand definitions will increase the reader's understanding of the text, while building vocabulary skills.

Sidebars: This boxed material within the main text allows readers to build knowledge, gain insights, explore possibilities, and broaden their perspectives by weaving together additional information to provide realistic and holistic perspectives.

Research Projects: Readers are pointed toward areas of further inquiry connected to each chapter. Suggestions are provided for projects that encourage deeper research and analysis.

Text-Dependent Questions: These questions send the reader back to the text for more careful attention to the evidence presented there.

Series Glossary of Key Terms: This back-of-the book glossary contains terminology used throughout this series. Words found here increase the reader's ability to read and comprehend higher-level books and articles in this field.

5

The Changing Face of the United States

Marian L. Smith, Historian
U.S. Citizenship and Immigration Services

Americans commonly assume that immigration today is very different than immigration of the past. The immigrants themselves appear to be unlike immigrants of earlier eras. Their language, their dress, their food, and their ways seem strange. At times people fear too many of these new immigrants will destroy the America they know. But has anything really changed? Do new immigrants have any different effect on America than old immigrants a century ago? Is the American fear of too much immigration a new development? Do immigrants really change America more than America changes the immigrants? The very subject of immigration raises many questions.

In the United States, immigration is more than a chapter in a history book. It is a continuous thread that links the present moment to the first settlers on North American shores. From the first colonists' arrival until today, immigrants have been met by Americans who both welcomed and feared them. Immigrant contributions were always welcome—on the farm, in the fields, and in the factories. Welcoming the poor, the persecuted, and the "huddled masses" became an American principle. Beginning with the original Pilgrims' flight from religious persecution in the 1600s, through the Irish migration to escape starvation in the 1800s, to the relocation of Central Americans seeking refuge from civil wars in the 1980s and 1990s, the United States has considered itself a haven for the destitute and the oppressed.

But there was also concern that immigrants would not adopt American ways, habits, or language. Too many immigrants might overwhelm America. If so, the dream of the Founding Fathers for United States government and society would be destroyed. For this reason, throughout American history some have argued that limiting or ending immigration is our patriotic duty. Benjamin Franklin feared there were so many German immigrants in Pennsylvania the Colonial Legislature would begin speaking German. "Progressive" leaders of the early 1900s feared that immigrants who could not read and understand the English language were not only exploited by "big business," but also served as the foundation for "machine politics" that undermined the U.S. Constitution. This theme continues today, usually voiced by those who bear no malice toward immigrants but who want to preserve American ideals.

Have immigrants changed? In colonial days, when most colonists were of English descent, they considered Germans, Swiss, and French immigrants as different. They were not "one of us" because they spoke a different language. Generations later, Americans of German or French descent viewed Polish, Italian, and Russian immigrants as strange. They were not "like us" because they had a different religion, or because they did not come from a tradition of constitutional government. Recently, Americans of Polish or Italian descent have seen Nicaraguan, Pakistani, or Vietnamese immigrants as too different to be included. It has long been said of American immigration that the latest ones to arrive usually want to close the door behind them.

It is important to remember that fear of individual immigrant groups seldom lasted, and always lessened. Benjamin Franklin's anxiety over German immigrants disappeared after those immigrants' sons and daughters helped the nation gain independence in the Revolutionary War. The Irish of the mid-1800s were among the most hated immigrants, but today we all wear green on St. Patrick's Day. While a century ago it was feared that Italian and other Catholic immigrants would vote as directed by the Pope, today that controversy is only a vague memory. Unfortunately, some ethnic groups continue their efforts to earn acceptance. The African

Americans' struggle continues, and some Asian Americans, whose families have been in America for generations, are the victims of current anti-immigrant sentiment.

Time changes both immigrants and America. Each wave of new immigrants, with their strange language and habits, eventually grows old and passes away. Their American-born children speak English. The immigrants' grandchildren are completely American. The strange foods of their ancestors—spaghetti, baklava, hummus, or tofu—become common in any American restaurant or grocery store. Much of what the immigrants brought to these shores is lost, principally their language. And what is gained becomes as American as St. Patrick's Day, Hanukkah, or Cinco de Mayo, and we forget that it was once something foreign.

Recent immigrants are all around us. They come from every corner of the earth to join in the American Dream. They will continue to help make the American Dream a reality, just as all the immigrants who came before them have done.

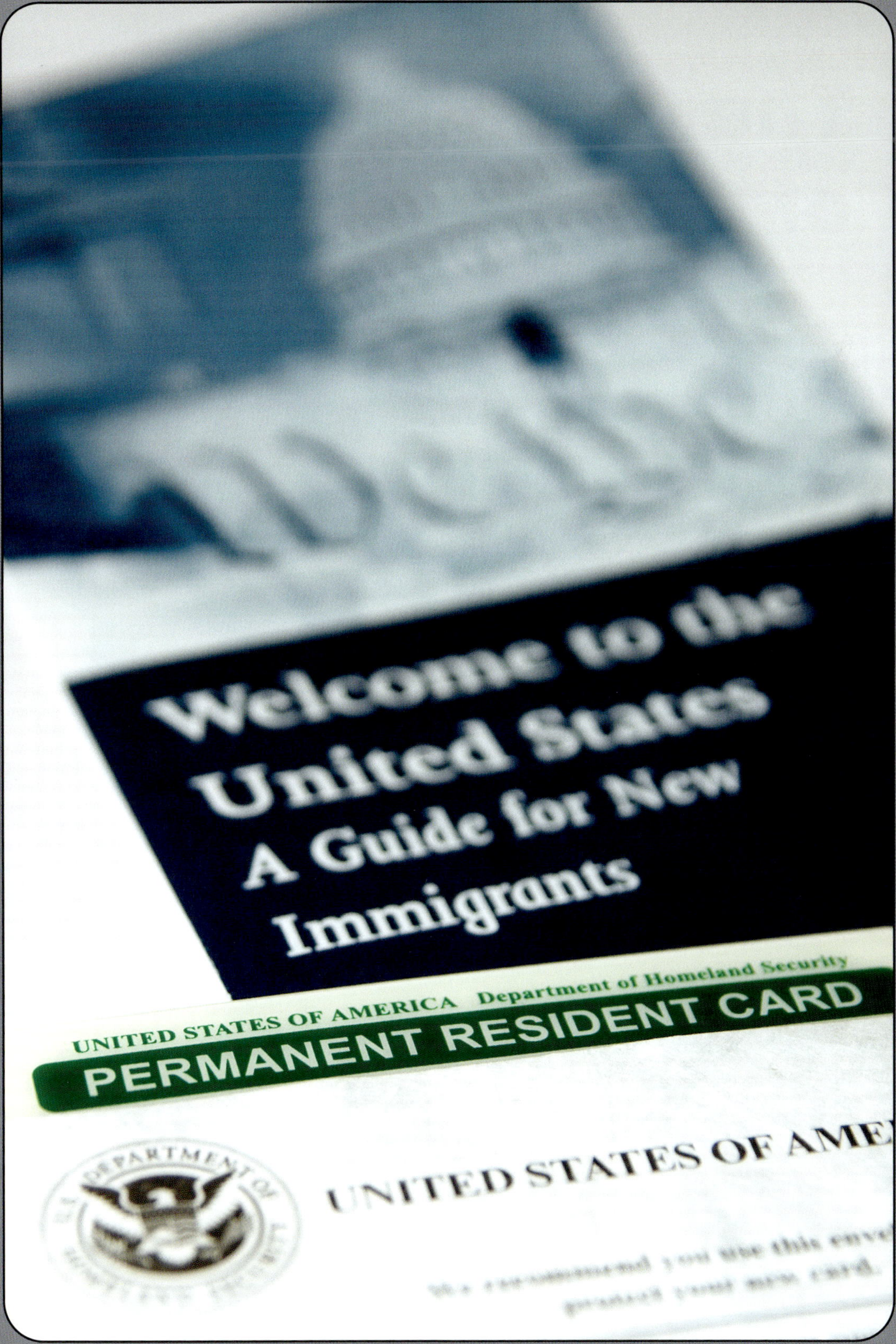
Welcome to the
United States
A Guide for New
Immigrants
UNITED STATES OF AMERICA Department of Homeland Security
PERMANENT RESIDENT CARD
UNITED STATES OF AME

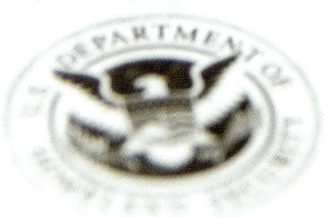

The Changing Face of Canada

Peter A. Hammerschmidt
former First Secretary, Permanent Mission of Canada to the United Nations

Throughout Canada's history, immigration has shaped and defined the very character of Canadian society. The migration of peoples from every part of the world into Canada has profoundly changed the way we look, speak, eat, and live. Through close and distant relatives who left their lands in search of a better life, all Canadians have links to immigrant pasts. We are a nation built by and of immigrants.

Two parallel forces have shaped the history of Canadian immigration. The enormous diversity of Canada's immigrant population is the most obvious. In the beginning came the enterprising settlers of the "New World," the French and English colonists. Soon after came the Scottish, Irish, and Northern and Central European farmers of the 1700s and 1800s. As the country expanded westward during the mid-1800s, migrant workers began arriving from China, Japan, and other Asian countries. And the turbulent twentieth century brought an even greater variety of immigrants to Canada, from the Caribbean, Africa, India, and Southeast Asia.

So while English- and French-Canadians are the largest ethnic groups in the country today, neither group alone represents a majority of the population. A large and vibrant multicultural mix makes up the rest, particularly in Canada's major cities. Toronto, Vancouver, and Montreal alone are home to people from over 200 ethnic groups!

Less obvious but equally important in the evolution of Canadian immigration has been hope. The promise of a better life lured Europeans and

Americans seeking cheap (sometimes even free) farmland. Thousands of Scots and Irish arrived to escape grinding poverty and starvation. Others came for freedom, to escape religious and political persecution. Canada has long been a haven to the world's dispossessed and disenfranchised—Dutch and German farmers cast out for their religious beliefs, black slaves fleeing the United States, and political refugees of despotic regimes in Europe, Africa, Asia, and South America.

The two forces of diversity and hope, so central to Canada's past, also shaped the modern era of Canadian immigration. Following the Second World War, Canada drew heavily on these influences to forge trailblazing immigration initiatives.

The catalyst for change was the adoption of the Canadian Bill of Rights in 1960. Recognizing its growing diversity and Canadians' changing attitudes towards racism, the government passed a federal statute barring discrimination on the grounds of race, national origin, color, religion, or sex. Effectively rejecting the discriminatory elements in Canadian immigration policy, the Bill of Rights forced the introduction of a new policy in 1962. The focus of immigration abruptly switched from national origin to the individual's potential contribution to Canadian society. The door to Canada was now open to every corner of the world.

Welcoming those seeking new hopes in a new land has also been a feature of Canadian immigration in the modern era. The focus on economic immigration has increased along with Canada's steadily growing economy, but political immigration has also been encouraged. Since 1945, Canada has admitted tens of thousands of displaced persons, including Jewish Holocaust survivors, victims of Soviet crackdowns in Hungary and Czechoslovakia, and refugees from political upheaval in Uganda, Chile, and Vietnam.

Prior to 1978, however, these political refugees were admitted as an exception to normal immigration procedures. That year, Canada revamped its refugee policy with a new Immigration Act that explicitly affirmed Canada's commitment to the resettlement of refugees from oppression. Today, the admission of refugees remains a central part of

Canadian immigration law and regulations.

Amendments to economic and political immigration policy have continued, refining further the bold steps taken during the modern era. Together, these initiatives have turned Canada into one of the world's few truly multicultural states.

Unlike the process of assimilation into a "melting pot" of cultures, immigrants to Canada are more likely to retain their cultural identity, beliefs, and practices. This is the source of some of Canada's greatest strengths as a society. And as a truly multicultural nation, diversity is not seen as a threat to Canadian identity. Quite the contrary—diversity is Canadian identity.

1 BEYOND GOLD MOUNTAIN

Just 100 years ago, the Chinese population in the United States was small, and most Chinese Americans lived in major cities. They had left their home in East Asia to earn their fortune in the land that many referred to as "Gold Mountain."

Today, Chinese immigrants and second- and third-generation Chinese Americans are spread across the length and breadth of the United States. The Chinese presence is significant in Canada as well.

Chinese immigrants today are more likely to dream of making their fortune with high-technology silicon rather than the gold that some of their ancestors discovered. Regardless, North America is still a land of great opportunity for many newcomers.

The People of China

Encompassing much of eastern Asia, China is the fourth-largest country in the world by area. Although it is slightly smaller than the United States, China contains more than four times as many people. It's the world's most populous country, home to an esti-

◀ The Great Wall of China, an ancient fortification that extends 1,500 miles (2,400 kilometers), is the country's most recognized landmark. Chinese immigrants have been leaving their home country for Canada and the United States since the 19th century; after living through periods of discrimination in both countries, the Chinese have become the largest immigrant group to Canada and the fourth largest to the United States.

mated 1.37 billion people as of January 2016. Officially known as the People's Republic of China, the country has 22 provinces, although the ruling government considers the island of Taiwan to be its 23rd province. China also contains five autonomous (or self-governing) regions, dominated by minority ethnic groups that have been allowed limited power (such as Tibet), and two special administrative regions—Hong Kong and Macau—which have their own executive, legislative, and judicial powers. The country's capital, Beijing, is one of four special municipalities.

People unfamiliar with China sometimes think it is an ethnically homogeneous country, but in fact it is home to many different minority groups. In addition to the more than 90 percent of the Chinese populace who belong to the Han ethnic group, there are 55 other groups recognized by the government, the largest of which include the Zhuang, Manchu, Hui, Miao, Uygur, Yi, Mongolian, Tibetan, Buyi, and Korean. Some of these minorities are concentrated in one region—the majority of Tibetans live in Tibet, for example—but others are dispersed throughout the whole country.

More than 70 percent of the Chinese speak Mandarin (Putonghua), the official language of China which originated in the north. The rest of the population speaks a number of Chinese dialects, which include Yue (Cantonese), Wu

Words to Understand in This Chapter

Cantonese—a Chinese dialect originating in Guangzhou (also called Canton), southern China's largest city.
Communist—a follower of communism, an economic and political system that advocates the elimination of private property and the equitable distribution of goods, and that usually claims the Communist Party has the sole right to govern.
enclave—a community that is culturally or ethnically different from the surrounding area.
homogeneous—having a uniform composition or structure.
Mandarin—the predominant dialect of China, spoken by over 70 percent of the population.

16 Chinese Immigrants

Chinese Influence on Western Medicine

China has the world's oldest living civilization, and some of its practices date back for many centuries. Acupuncture is one traditional Chinese discipline in the field of health and medicine that has increasingly been adopted by non-Chinese people.

Acupuncture is an ancient Chinese method of relieving pain and treating disease by inserting needles into specific areas of the body. Acupuncturists believe that pain and disease are caused by imbalances in the body between the two principal forces of nature known as *yin* and *yang*. Ailments occur when one force is stronger than the other; acupuncture is a method of equalizing the balance between these forces.

Practiced throughout Asia and Europe, acupuncture has gained acceptance with many people in the United States and Canada. Some members of the medical profession find that acupuncture is useful as a supplement to Western medicine; others find it to be an acceptable alternative in its own right. Most U.S. states and Canadian provinces regulate and grant licenses to establishments that offer acupuncture.

(Shanghaiese), Minbei (Fuzhou), Minnan (Hokkien-Taiwanese), Xiang, Gan, and Hakka.

As is common with many Communist countries throughout history, China is officially atheist and claims no national religion. However, an estimated 250 million Chinese practice Buddhism or Taoism, with perhaps 70 million more following Christianity and about 25 million adhering to Islam.

One of the Largest Immigrant Groups

In 2013 the United States received more legal immigrants from China (over 68,000) than from any other country except Mexico. That same year, Chinese made up the largest group of new immigrants to Canada, with about 34,000 arriving.

In 2010, according to the U.S. census, more than 3.3 million residents of the United States claimed Chinese ancestry alone. That made Chinese the largest single group of Asian Americans; they accounted for more than 20 percent of the U.S. Asian population.

The number of people of Chinese ancestry living in Canada

Beyond Gold Mountain 17

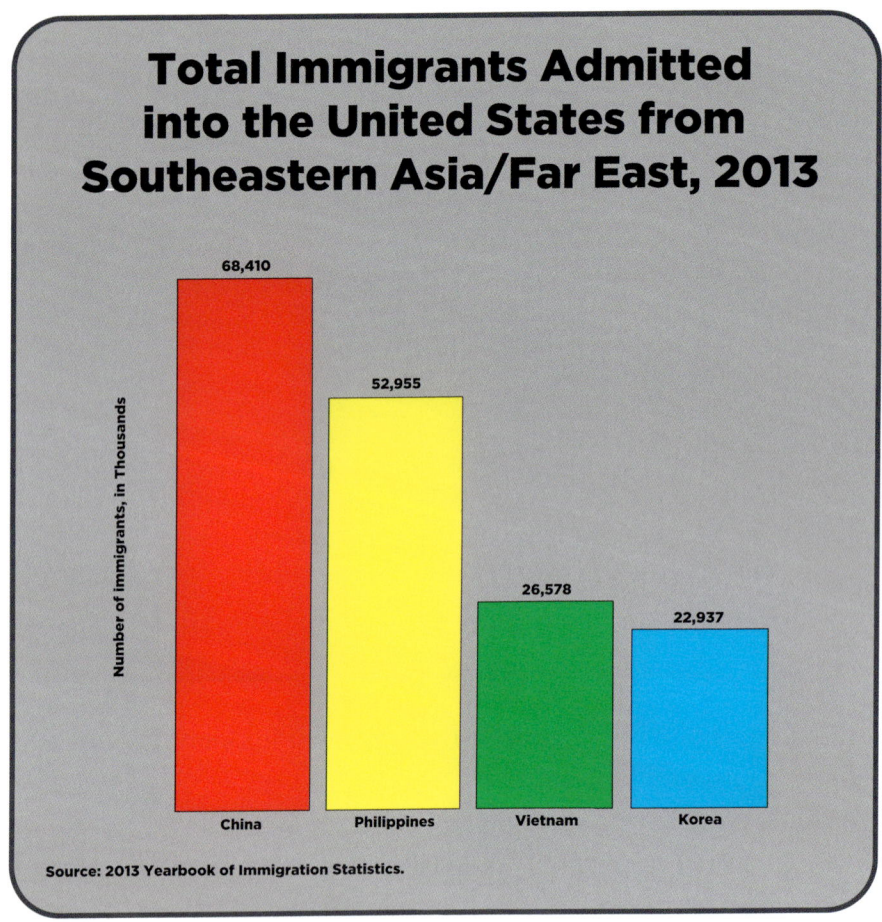

has also increased significantly in recent years. According to Canada's 2011 National Household Survey (NHS), Chinese Canadians numbered more than 1.3 million—or 4 percent of Canada's total population. That was up from about 1 percent in 2001. NHS data revealed that Chinese constituted Canada's second-largest "visible minority group"—defined as "persons, other than Aboriginal persons, who are non-Caucasian in race or non-white in colour"—behind only South Asians.

Growing Migration Numbers

The path from China to North America has often been harrowing, causing many difficulties for those looking to immigrate. Many have died or have had to return to their homeland before they made it to their destination. Some of the obstacles have been placed by the homeland government, some by destination countries, and some by the choppy seas along the travel route. On the other hand, many Chinese immigrants have enjoyed a comfortable and modern jet trip to Toronto, Los Angeles, or New York.

But no matter how they have reached the continent, Chinese immigrants have continued to come to North America in large numbers. Each day in 2013, for example, the United States and Canada combined to welcome an average of 280 new legal immigrants from China. Undocumented immigrants have added to that total, though their numbers are hard to determine. What is certain is that Chinese Americans and Chinese Canadians will continue to play a vital role in the economic and cultural life of their adopted countries.

Text-Dependent Questions

1. What is acupuncture?
2. What is the official language of China?
3. What's the largest "visible minority group" in Canada? Where do Chinese rank?

Research Project

Using a library or the Internet, research one of China's provinces or autonomous regions. In a box, present the following basic information: Total area; Highest point; Lowest point; Population; Capital city; Other major cities. Then write a three- or four- paragraph essay on unique aspects or special issues facing the province or autonomous region.

Beyond Gold Mountain   19

2 A Brief History of Modern China

During the 19th and early 20th centuries, China endured decades of economic hardship and the intervention of foreign powers, in particular Japan, which continually sought to gain control of Chinese land. The second half of the 20th century was marked by revolution and internal friction. China has emerged as a global economic powerhouse in the 21st century. However, its government is repressive and plagued by corruption, according to human-rights organizations and independent journalists.

End of the Dynastic System

For more than two millennia, China was ruled by a succession of dynasties. By the early 20th century, however, the ruling Qing dynasty was corrupt, weak, and unpopular.

In October 1911, revolutionaries inspired by a doctor named Sun Yat-sen (whose name is also transliterated as Sun Zhongshan) defeated Qing forces in the city of Wuhan, in central China's Hubei Province. Sun dreamed of a democratic China. He championed reform of landownership practices that kept millions of Chinese peasants landless and impoverished.

From Wuhan, the revolution spread quickly. Soon, two-thirds of China's provinces—covering the southern, southwest-

◀ One of the most influential leaders of the 20th century, Mao Zedong (1893–1976) was founder of the People's Republic of China, established in 1949. As the leader of the Communist Revolution in the 1940s and chairman of the Communist Party, Mao was a pivotal force behind the political and economic transformation of China.

ern, and central parts of the country—had thrown off Qing rule and declared themselves independent. In late December 1911, representatives of 17 provinces convened in the city of Nanjing and formally established the Republic of China. The representatives elected Sun Yat-sen as its provisional president.

In northern China, though, the Qing dynasty clung to power. Militarily, the Republic of China wasn't in a position to conquer the remaining Qing-controlled territory. A Qing general, Yuan Shikai, offered a solution. In exchange for his being named provisional president of the Republic of China, Yuan promised to get the Qing emperor to abdicate (give up the throne). Reluctantly, Sun Yat-sen and other officials of the new Chinese republic agreed to the arrangement. On February 12, 1912, six-year-old Emperor Puyi was compelled to abdicate, ending the 267-year reign of the Qing dynasty. Yuan Shikai took over as provisional president of the Republic of China.

In late 1912 and early 1913, elections were held for a two-chamber legislature, the National Assembly. The Kuomintang (also spelled Guomindang), or Nationalist Party, won the most seats. But its leader was assassinated—probably on orders from Yuan Shikai—before the National Assembly had been seated in Beijing. When the assembly did convene, Yuan forced its members, under the threat of imprisonment, to elect him to a five-

Words to Understand in This Chapter

demographic—relating to the dynamic balance of a population, especially its capacity for expansion or decline.

gross domestic product (GDP)—an economic indicator that measures the total value of goods and services produced in a country during a one-year period.

guerrilla—a member of a usually small group of soldiers who don't belong to a regular army and who fight as an independent unit; relating to the irregular tactics used by such a group.

purge—to remove someone from a political party or government.

reactionary—opposing political or social reform; an ultraconservative person.

year term as the Republic of China's regular president. He then banned the Nationalist Party and, in January 1914, dissolved the National Assembly.

Sun Yat-sen tried to direct another revolution, this one aimed at overthrowing Yuan Shikai, with the Kuomintang forming the backbone of the opposition. But a series of uprisings failed miserably. In December 1915, Yuan declared himself emperor of the "Chinese Empire." But he soon lost control of his military forces and was compelled to give up his reign as emperor. In June 1916, he died.

Power Struggle

Following Yuan Shikai's death, China descended into political chaos. Warlords took control of large sections of the country, battling one another for territory and for the reins of the central government in Beijing.

Dr. Sun Yat-Sen was provisional president of the Republic of China from January 1, 1912, to March 10, 1912. Yuan Shikai, who controlled an army, seized power on March 10, 1912.

In 1921, the Chinese Communist Party (CCP) was founded. Inspired by the success of the Russian Revolution—which overthrew Russia's monarchy and ultimately led to the establishment of the Soviet Union, the world's first Communist state—the CCP's members hoped to lead a revolution in China.

By 1924, Sun Yat-sen had decided that the Kuomintang should make common cause with the CCP. He died the following year, but the Nationalist-Communist alliance survived—at least for a while.

In July 1926, the Nationalists and Communists began a military campaign against China's warlords. It was known as the Northern Expedition. Chiang Kai-shek (also known as Jiang

A Brief History of Modern China

A Chinese Communist army, which fought against the Kuomintang for control of the country.

Jieshi), the Kuomintang's most prominent general, led the 90,000-man National Revolutionary Army north from the city of Guangzhou (formerly known as Canton). Meanwhile, Communists began organizing peasants to fight in the countryside and labor unions to rise up in cities.

Chiang's army, which had Soviet advisors and arms, was better organized and equipped than the private armies of the warlords. In addition, the brutality with which the warlords ruled their territories made ordinary Chinese eager to get rid of them. Tens of thousands of peasants swelled the ranks of the National Revolutionary Army as it marched north. As a result of these factors and of Communist organizing efforts, the Northern Expedition made rapid progress. Within nine months, the National Revolutionary Army had advanced some 950 miles (1,530 km), to the Yangtze River. It now controlled about half of China.

But there was friction within the Kuomintang leadership. In early 1927, a left-wing faction closely allied with the CCP set up what it claimed was the official Nationalist government in Wuhan, a city Chiang Kai-shek's army had liberated before moving on to Nanchang. The Wuhan leaders secretly planned to arrest Chiang, but he got wind of the plot.

In April, Chiang marched into Shanghai, where Communists and allied labor-union militias had recently ousted the local warlord forces and set up a provisional government. On April 12, under Chiang's orders, Communists in Shanghai were rounded up and massacred.

Soon Chinese Communists also found themselves under attack from their erstwhile allies in Wuhan. That happened after the Nationalists uncovered a CCP plan to seize control of the Wuhan government.

Chiang Kai-shek organized a rival Nationalist government in Nanjing. When the Wuhan government fell apart, Chiang became the undisputed leader of the Kuomintang.

The CCP had established its own fighting force, known popularly as the Red Army, and in August and September 1927 it struck Chiang's forces in several provinces. The uprisings, however, were put down. A long civil war between the Nationalists and the Communists had begun.

While suppressing the Communists, Chiang resumed the push northward to defeat China's warlords. In 1928, his forces took Beijing and effectively unified the country. The Nationalist regime received international recognition as the sole legitimate government of China.

Japanese Invasions and World War II

In September 1931, Japanese forces invaded Manchuria, in northeastern China. Japan conquered the region and set up a puppet regime there.

Chiang Kai-shek seemed more intent on defeating the Chinese Communist Party than on trying to expel the Japanese from Manchuria. Chiang's forces inflicted heavy losses on the

Communists but were unable to eradicate them.

By October 1934, the Nationalists appeared to have the main formation of the Red Army—more than 85,000 strong—encircled in southeastern China's Jiangxi Province. But the Communists broke out, and in a yearlong retreat covering more than 7,500 miles (12,070 km), about 8,000 escaped to Shaanxi Province in northern China. It was during this retreat, known appropriately as the Long March, that Mao Zedong emerged as the CCP's paramount leader.

The Communists relied on support from peasants in the countryside. They used guerrilla tactics to neutralize the advantages enjoyed by Chiang's forces, including numerical superiority and better weaponry.

In December 1936, two Nationalist generals seized Chiang Kai-shek. They demanded that Chiang stop fighting the Communists and concentrate on fighting the Japanese instead. He agreed and was released.

The Nationalists and Communists formed a unified front against the Japanese. That became especially important after 1937, when Japan launched a large-scale invasion of China. Over the ensuing years, Japanese forces conquered and occupied a significant portion of coastal China. But they were unable to penetrate into the country's rugged interior or fully quell Chinese opposition. Chiang had removed the Nationalist government to remote Chongqing, which was ravaged by Japanese bombers but remained beyond the reach of ground troops.

In December 1941, Japanese attacks against British interests in Asia and against the U.S. naval base in Pearl Harbor, Hawaii, drew the United Kingdom and the United States into war with Japan—and opened up a sprawling new theater in World War II. China, which had been receiving aid from the United States, officially joined the Allies.

Japan finally surrendered in the summer of 1945, bringing World War II to an end. It's impossible to know precisely how many Chinese died as a result of their country's eight-year struggle against the Japanese occupation, but the toll is staggering.

Two Chinese men kneel prior to execution by Japanese soldiers. From 1937 to 1945, the Chinese fought against a Japanese invasion, while also waging a civil war between the Nationalists and Communists.

Recent estimates put the number around 14 million.

Victory of the Communists

In the latter stages of World War II especially, the alliance between the Nationalists and the Chinese Communist Party showed signs of fraying. And after the war against Japan was over, the two sides resumed their civil war in earnest.

At first, the Nationalists controlled China's major cities. But the Communists held rural areas, especially in North China. The United States tried to mediate a peace agreement between the two parties, but the effort ultimately proved unsuccessful.

With support from the Soviet Union, the Chinese Communists began making gains. They won support from

A Brief History of Modern China 27

China's peasants, in part because Chiang's Nationalist troops often mistreated and brutalized the civilian population.

By 1948, the tide of the conflict had begun turning decisively in favor of the Communists. They took a number of important cities. Nationalist soldiers deserted in droves. In January 1949, Beijing fell to the Communists.

Chiang's last hope was to hold a defensive line on the southern banks of the Yangtze River. But in April 1949, Communist forces breached that line. By year's end, the remnants of the Nationalist army, along with several hundred thousand civilians, had fled to the island of Taiwan, where the Republic of China government was transferred. It remained headed by Chiang Kai-shek and the Nationalists. They claimed the Republic of China was the legitimate government of all China, and the United States and the United Nations recognized that claim.

Meanwhile, on October 1, 1949, Mao Zedong proclaimed the establishment of the People's Republic of China (PRC). It, too, claimed to be China's legitimate government. In the PRC, as

 Controversy over Tibet

Home to the world's tallest peak, Mount Everest, the mountainous region of Tibet has been under the control of China for more than six decades. One of the least developed regions in China, Tibet is particularly hard hit during times of famine.

Before the Chinese invaded Tibet, it was run by a religious government of Buddhist spiritual leaders whose two central figures were the Panchen Lama and the Dalai Lama. In 1951 Tibet surrendered its authority to the Chinese, although it kept its right to regional self-government.

For decades the Dalai Lama, whom his followers consider the reincarnation of the Buddha of Compassion, has maintained a Tibetan government in exile, and through nonviolent means has pressured the People's Republic of China to give Tibet the same status as that granted to Hong Kong (a special administrative region with its own executive, legislative, and judicial powers). Meanwhile, the Chinese government has suppressed Tibetan Buddhism by closing or destroying monasteries, and arresting or persecuting monks, nuns, and other separatists. Tibetan separatism has gained support in the West from those who argue that China is abusing Tibetans' basic human rights and their right to religious freedom. Although China's rule over Tibet is controversial, the region remains firmly a part of the People's Republic of China.

28 Chinese Immigrants

in other Communist countries, the government and the Communist Party were essentially one and the same. The Chinese Communist Party maintained that it alone had the right to govern. As chairman of the Chinese Communist Party, Mao was China's paramount leader.

Turbulent Times

More than a decade of war had left China devastated. One of the first priorities of the new Communist government was to stabilize the economy and restore production. But Mao and other top officials of the ruling Chinese Communist Party also made sure to consolidate their power by eliminating opponents, including Nationalist supporters, wealthy landlords, and critics of communism. The "Campaign to Suppress Counterrevolutionaries," which got under way in early 1950, would last three years and claim an estimated 2 million lives.

By 1956, however, Mao Zedong signaled that the Chinese Communist Party was ready to tolerate some freedom of expression. In fact, in what came to be called the Hundred Flowers Movement, Mao even encouraged citizens to criticize the government in order to make it better. "Let a hundred flowers bloom," Mao proclaimed, echoing a famous Chinese saying, "and a hundred schools of thought contend."

Many Chinese, especially professors, students, and intellectuals, took Mao at his word. They publicly—and often harshly—criticized the government and its policies. These critics would soon regret sharing their views. By 1957, the "hundred flowers" had withered, and in July of that year Mao launched the so-called Anti-Rightist Campaign. Half a million people who had criticized the government were rounded up. Some were executed; others were tortured or sentenced to long terms in labor camps.

In late 1957, Mao outlined a plan to put Communist principles into practice and transform China into one of the world's leading industrial powers. The effort, known as the Great Leap Forward, would abolish private ownership of land and force peasants onto massive "people's communes," where they would live together, study communism together, and work the fields together. The communes would be under the overall direction of Communist Party officials.

Mao and other CCP leaders were confident the commune system would dramatically increase crop yields. And the government had plans for the projected surpluses. After sufficient grain had been distributed to China's cities to feed the people there, the remainder would be exported, to help pay for the equipment China needed to carry out its program of rapid industrialization.

But the Great Leap Forward was beset by fundamental problems. To begin, commune workers all received the same wages regardless of how hard they worked. So a major incentive for working hard was removed. Additionally, commune managers were chosen primarily for their loyalty to the Communist Party rather than for their ability. Many were incompetent. Yet they had strong incentives to report good news to their superiors in Beijing.

Beginning in 1958, commune managers reported record harvests throughout China. The actual crop yields, however, were average or below average. But the amount of grain the government took from the communes was based on the inflated figures. This resulted in food shortages on the communes. The situation was repeated the following year, by which time a full-fledged famine was sweeping across rural China.

But even as the crisis deepened, Chairman Mao and other top CCP officials refused to change course. They insisted that there was no famine, and any apparent food shortages in rural China were caused by disloyal peasants hoarding food for themselves. On many communes, Communist Party officials beat and tortured peasants in an effort to get them to reveal where their caches of stolen grain were located—but of course there were no hidden supplies of grain.

By the hundreds of thousands, starving peasants wandered off their communes in a desperate search for food. Untold numbers died along roadsides and in fields, and in many places the corpses were left to decompose where they'd fallen, as no one was around to bury them.

In 1961, Mao and the CCP leadership finally abandoned the Great Leap Forward. By that time, however, the Chinese people had endured unspeakable suffering. Estimates of the number who starved to death range from about 15 million to 40 million.

The Cultural Revolution

After the disaster wrought by the Great Leap Forward, Mao Zedong's influence waned. He remained chairman of the CCP, but other Party officials took the lead in governing the country. They reversed some of Mao's policies—for example, by permitting peasant families to cultivate small, private plots of land for their own benefit, and by limiting the economic importance of the "people's communes." Such measures were intended to help China's economy recover and to ease the plight of the country's peasants.

But Mao apparently regarded these developments as a repudiation of his leadership. And he was not content to remain on the sidelines as others charted China's course.

In 1966, Mao used an obscure literary controversy to mount a political comeback. A circular he drafted asserted that enemies of communism—"a bunch of counter-revolutionary revisionists," as he called them—had "sneaked into the party, the government, the army, and various cultural circles. . . . Once conditions are ripe, they will seize political power."

Claiming his main rivals in the CCP were among the "counter-revolutionary revisionists," Mao successfully had them purged. Once again he stood as China's unquestioned leader.

But the Cultural Revolution was only beginning. In Beijing, a group of high school students fanatically devoted to the CCP chairman had organized themselves into the "Red Guards of Mao's Thought." Mao encouraged other high school and university students across the country to form their own Red Guards units. And he incited these young followers to root out China's "hidden enemies."

In front of a poster of Chairman Mao Zedong, a group of Chinese schoolchildren read from the "Little Red Book," the nickname for the famous book of quotations by Mao. Public readings like this one were common during the Cultural Revolution (1966–76), a national movement launched to make Chinese society more uniformly Communist.

The Red Guards wreaked havoc in their schools. Reciting excerpts from Quotations from Chairman Mao—a slim volume of sayings commonly known as the Little Red Book—they humiliated, beat, and sometimes killed teachers and administrators for holding "erroneous ideas" and other supposed offenses.

The Cultural Revolution quickly engulfed all of Chinese society. Factory workers denounced their managers. Children turned on their parents. Neighbors accused neighbors. And the Red Guards meted out punishment.

Millions of Chinese, particularly intellectuals and those in positions of authority, lived in abject terror. A misinterpreted comment, a perceived slight, or a petty jealousy might cause someone to level charges of "counter-revolutionary sympathies." And that, in turn, would prompt a visit from the Red Guards—and very likely a vicious beating, a long sentence in a rural labor camp for "reeducation," or a violent death.

It's nearly impossible to overstate the disruption caused by the Cultural Revolution. Millions of Chinese children lost out on an education—first, because so many teachers were denounced and removed that schools had to be shuttered, and then, because the government took at least one child from every urban family and sent that child to work on a rural commune. Industrial production plummeted because engineers and managers were removed from their jobs wholesale for placing "technical expertise" above "correct political thinking." Food shortages again became widespread, and many thousands of Chinese starved to death. Many others tried to flee China, even though it was illegal to do so. Some of them found sanctuary in the United States and Canada.

The Cultural Revolution lasted a decade, finally coming to an end after Mao Zedong's death. But by 1967, Mao had already moved to limit the chaos he'd unleashed. He ordered China's army, the People's Liberation Army (PLA), to clamp down on the most radical Red Guards groups. Brutal, bloody clashes ensued, and in some areas large numbers of captured Red Guards members were executed. By mid-1968, the PLA had fully suppressed the Red Guards.

To this day, scholars debate Mao's actions and motives during the Cultural Revolution. Some believe he launched the Cultural Revolution primarily as a means of regaining the political power he'd lost. Others claim he was motivated by a genuine concern that reactionary elements in Chinese government and society might betray the Communist revolution. Critics insist that Mao was fully aware of the horrors committed during the Cultural Revolution, including the torture and murder of untold numbers of innocent people (the overall death toll is believed to be 1.5 million or more). Apologists, though, claim that Mao's subordinates in the Communist Party kept many details from the chairman, in order to appear supportive of his program and thereby advance their own careers.

Mao was also influenced by the so-called Gang of Four, which included his wife Jiang Qing and three of her followers—Wang Hongwen, Yao Wenyuan, and Zhang Chunqiao. Through their involvement in propaganda and the national arts, these four influential leaders made grabs for power while attempting to bring every aspect of Chinese life under Communist control.

In 1971, the United Nations voted to recognize the People's Republic of China, rather than the Taiwan-based Republic of China, as China's legitimate government. The vote followed an announcement by Richard Nixon, the U.S. president, of a pending visit to the People's Republic. Nixon's February 1972 trip signaled an improvement in U.S.-China relations. However, little changed for the Chinese people under the Communist regime. In her book *Asian American Experiences in the United States*, author Joann Faung Jean Lee interviewed Chinese immigrant Kenny Lai about why he chose to leave China in the early 1970s. He explained:

> [F]or those of us who had no connections, we could plan on spending the rest of our lives there [on a farm commune]. I thought that as long as I didn't marry, maybe I could withstand it. I could stand spending the next forty to fifty years on the commune. But I was thinking when I got married, my children would be forced to stay there, and my children's children. So future generations would be forced to be farmers. So there was no way out. If they wouldn't let me leave, the only thing to do was escape.

Almost all Chinese immigrants to the United States, Canada, or other countries during the early 1970s believed that by leaving China they had escaped a horrible fate not only for themselves but for their children and grandchildren.

In 1976, Chairman Mao died. Upon his death, many Chinese people felt a sense of shock and loss that is hard for most Westerners to understand. Although Mao had been responsible for policies that killed millions of Chinese people, he had also helped develop the national identity of Communist China. Over the years his sayings had become a part of common speech. And

Jiang Qing (1914–91), wife of Mao Zedong, stands trial in 1981. Jiang was a member of the infamous Gang of Four that was tried and convicted of treason during the administration of Deng Xiaoping. Many people believed that the gang's imprisonment was proof that the Cultural Revolution had ended.

the Chinese Communist Party maintained a massive propaganda effort to portray Mao as "the Great Helmsman," who had expertly and effectively guided the country. The period after his death was marked by profound uncertainty for most people living in China.

Deng Xiaoping and the "Four Modernizations"

Shortly after Mao's death, Hua Guofeng became Communist Party chairman. He had already become China's premier following the death of Premier Zhou Enlai in January 1976. Determined that the Chinese government not remain under the thumb of the Gang of Four, Hua had them arrested. Their imprisonment meant the end of their power in China, as well as the end of the Cultural Revolution. Each of the four leaders was sentenced to death, though the sentences were later reduced to life imprisonment.

By the early 1980s Hua had been replaced by Deng Xiaoping, who had strong ideas about how to improve the economic situation of the Chinese people. In the early 1960s, when Premier Zhou had called for the modernization of four sectors—agriculture, industry, defense, and science and technology—the Cultural Revolution had swept away his efforts. In 1975, Zhou tried again to institute reforms with the help of Deng, at that time recently "rehabilitated" and returned to political life after being forced into a rural prison camp. Finally, after the arrest of the Gang of Four, Deng was able to incorporate the plans for the "Four Modernizations" into official state policy. Deng gradually opened up China to foreign trade and investment. He also started dismantling China's commune system. He introduced market-based economic reforms, steering the country away from

U.S. President Jimmy Carter (right) and Premier Deng Xiaoping speak at a press conference in Washington, D.C., January 1979. Later that year China and the United States established full diplomatic relations, one of many steps toward reconciliation that first began with President Richard Nixon's 1972 visit to China.

the central planning characteristic of a Communist economy. By the mid-1980s, China's economy had begun taking off. Since then, economists say, more than 600 million Chinese have been lifted out of extreme poverty.

In spite of his economic reforms, however, Deng showed no inclination to grant the Chinese people greater political rights. He also continued to suppress religious freedom.

Deng Xiaoping was in some ways a more personable leader than Mao. He was less revered but more liked. He was even affectionately addressed by his first name in some student parades, and his statements of daily philosophy were popular, but by no means as treasured as the sayings of Chairman Mao.

China's One-Child Policy

One of the major differences between Mao and Deng's policies stemmed from their different attitudes toward China's population. During the early years of Mao's administration, the Chinese government favored high population growth. Despite the country's many widespread famines, Mao and his ministers believed that large families were necessary in order to provide as many workers as possible for the Chinese economy. Moreover, in traditional peasant societies large families served a practical function, as their members would provide for each other and assist elders who would someday be unavailable to work.

The policy of encouraging China's citizens to have large families remained in place for a few years after Mao's death. But as Deng became confident in his leadership, his government began to evaluate how it could feed its millions—and determined that it could not. As a result the Chinese government decided to attempt to solve the crisis by persuading its citizens to have smaller families.

The plan remained in place during the 1970s, and in 1980 was codified into what became known as the "one-child policy." According to the new standards, Chinese couples were allowed to have only one child, and the Chinese government took severe measures to make sure this policy was followed. In many provinces, women were forced to undergo late-term abortions and sterilizations. All pregnant women had to have *shengyu zheng*, or birthing licenses, with them when they went to the hospitals to deliver their babies.

Human rights groups denounced China's one-child policy—which the government enforced with a variety of coercive and even violent tactics—as a fundamental violation of individual autonomy. But many Chinese saw the policy as a necessary measure to keep the burgeoning population under control and thus minimize hunger, poverty, and other social ills.

The one-child policy had unforeseen consequences, however. In Chinese culture, families attach great importance to having a son. Because they were only permitted one child, many couples aborted female fetuses. The result was a massive gender imbalance—in 2000, for example, there were 120 male babies born in China for every 100 female babies—meaning tens of millions of Chinese men will never be able to marry.

Another consequence of China's one-child policy is a steadily aging population. The United Nations' Department of Economic and Social Affairs projected that the percentage of Chinese over 60 years old would grow from 16.8 percent in 2014 to 45.4 percent 2050. And in 2014, for the third year in a row, the size of China's working-age population shrank. These trends present a huge challenge: How can China sustain economic growth over the long run with fewer workers and many more old people to support?

That consideration helped spur the Chinese government to change its one-child policy. In 2013, the government announced that any married couple in which the husband or the wife was an only child would be permitted to have two children. Two years later, in 2015, the government decided that all Chinese couples could have two children. That change should eventually ease, but cannot completely erase, China's demographic problems. More than three decades of the one-child policy will have a dramatic and continuing impact on the makeup of China's population.

Many Chinese families today have only one child, in accordance with a government policy introduced during the early 1980s. The one-child law, controversial among many international human rights groups, was designed to limit China's population size.

The Chinese government's involvement in the reproductive decisions of its citizens reflects a larger reality. The right of privacy has been almost entirely lacking in Communist China. In the towns, village elders keep track of any infractions committed by residents. In the cities, each person is monitored by a street committee, which keeps track of sanitation, traffic, birth control, and the general behavior of citizens. This repressive system of scrutiny and prosecution has been a primary reason why Chinese people have decided to leave their homeland.

Tiananmen Square Democracy Movement

By the late 1980s, Chinese who were of college age or younger had few if any detailed recollections of the Cultural Revolution. Unlike their elders, they had limited knowledge of how ruthlessly the government was apt to treat actual critics and even suspected opponents.

Young dissidents, mostly university students in Beijing, began a large-scale protest in the city's Tiananmen Square on April 15, 1989. Their demands were many: They wanted to be able to choose their leaders, rather than having them selected from among veteran party leaders, by the veteran party leaders themselves. They sought the freedom to organize and the right to express their beliefs. They also called for an end to government corruption, an improvement of the educational system, and leniency for previous victims of political persecution.

The Communist government interpreted the students' demands and the growing democracy movement as a threat to its own power. On June 4, government soldiers and tanks entered the square, killing hundreds and injuring thousands of the demonstrators. Thousands more fled in fear for their lives. Some were captured and imprisoned, while others made it out of the country, later settling in North America, Australia, Europe, or other parts of Asia.

The Tiananmen Square incident shocked the Chinese people, making them even more distrustful of their government. Many decided to leave the country by whatever means possible, and emigration from China—both legal and illegal—increased in numbers that would have been unheard of in the 1960s or even the 1980s.

Continuing Economic Reforms

After Deng Xiaoping died in 1997, Jiang Zemin became the leader of the Communist Party in China. He was the first supreme leader in almost 100 years who did not owe his rise to power to military intervention or control. Although Jiang still had close ties to the People's Liberation Army, he also under-

Tiananmen Square, located in the Chinese capital of Beijing, was the site of the June 1989 massacre of hundreds of student protesters. The demonstrators had made demands for more democratic freedoms, which the communist leadership perceived as a threat to the government's power.

stood how to achieve his goals through political means rather than exclusively through military force.

Jiang continued to follow the economic policies initiated under Deng. In the early 1990s, after realizing that it could not succeed economically under a strict Communist system, the government made changes. It allowed for the privatization of some of the farming communes and then of some businesses and factories. The Communist Party characterized this economic system as

Chinese-style communism, but in fact the system bore a number of similarities to a free-market economy.

The Chinese people responded positively to the changes. Businessman Robert Lawrence Kuhn described the results in his book *Made in China*, published in 2000: "By the 1990s, in the full flush of reform, it was a common joke that *all* Chinese people were going into business. 'Jumping into the sea' was the operant metaphor—a phrase that captures the excitement and uncertainty of the market economy."

Jiang Zemin's successors, Hu Jintao (who was China's top leader from 2002 to 2012) and Xi Jinping (who took the reins of power in 2012), continued the country's move toward a more market-based, capitalistic economy. The results have been astounding. In 1978, when Deng Xiaoping initiated his first economic reforms, China's gross domestic product (GDP) stood at slightly over $215 billion. By 2014 it topped $10.3 trillion.

Zhang Boli's Escape from China

Growing up in China during the 1960s, a decade of misery, terror, and famine, Zhang Boli was well acquainted with death. "Almost every day, people died of starvation in the surrounding villages," he states in his memoir *Escape from China: The Long Journey From Tiananmen to Freedom*, published in 2002. But he was horrified to learn later that people living in other regions had experienced far worse conditions. "[W]hen I became a reporter, I learned that the area where I lived was among those with the smallest number of deaths caused by famine," he recalled. His outrage at the conditions of the Chinese peasants during his childhood led him to actively protest against the Communist government.

As a leader in the Tiananmen Square Democracy Movement, 26-year-old Zhang, along with fellow students Guo Haifeng and Bai Meng, led the marchers into the square. The students believed that the government would be caught off-guard by the protest and would not initiate violence against them, a belief Zhang later realized was naive.

After the massacre on June 4, thousands of students fled the square. Twenty-one of them soon learned that they, including Zhang, had been placed on the Chinese government's "Most Wanted" list. After spending two years as a fugitive in rural northeastern China, Zhang was eventually smuggled into Hong Kong. From there he made his way to the United States, where he has worked as a Christian minister and public speaker.

Xi Jinping, president of the People's Republic of China, addresses the United Nations in September 2015.

Depending on how it's measured, China either has the world's largest economy, or is second only to the United States. But there are more than four times as many Chinese people as there are Americans. In income per capita (per person), China still isn't wealthy; in fact, it ranks near the middle of the world's countries.

According to many China scholars, the country's leaders—from Deng Xiaoping to Xi Jinping—have understood that the Chinese people will generally tolerate the Communist Party's monopoly on power as long as their material circumstances continue to improve. In other words, ordinary Chinese will accept a lack of political freedom in exchange for tangible economic benefits.

That calculation may be tested in the coming years. In 2015, China's economy grew at its slowest pace in a quarter century, and many experts were predicting a prolonged period of slower growth—and even a potential economic crisis. "The relentless economic slowdown and the unfolding panic in China's financial markets have blasted apart several long-cherished myths," the Shanghai-born political scientist Minxin Pei wrote in February 2016. "One of them is that of a competent autocratic regime run by clever technocrats and decisive politicians. Recent stumbles by Beijing . . . demonstrate that Chinese technocrats may not be as clever as many thought. As for the country's politicians, they appear to be decisive, but only in making bad calls."

A deteriorating economy may or may not ultimately lead to a reckoning for the Chinese Communist Party. But it was never the case that all Chinese citizens were willing to trade political rights and freedoms for increased prosperity. And for many who desire more personal freedom, the idea of emigrating holds significant appeal.

Chinese workers assemble electronics in a factory in the Shenzhen economic zone. Thanks to low wages and a large workforce, China has developed a manufacturing economy.

Hong Kong and Taiwan

From 1841 to 1997—with the exception of a four-year Japanese occupation during World War II—Hong Kong was under British control. In the 1980s, China and Britain began negotiating its return to China. Although China had ceded the island of Hong Kong to Britain after being defeated in a conflict known as the First Opium War (1839–42), the British had leased the adjacent Kowloon Peninsula and New Territories. With the lease set to expire in 1997, British officials decided to hand over Hong Kong as well. An acceptable arrangement was devised by Deng Xiaoping. It was known as "One Country, Two Systems." Under this arrangement, Hong Kong would become part of China but would, for a period of 50 years, be allowed to keep its capitalist economy and its political system, which included democratic elements such as a popularly elected legislature. Hong Kong residents would be guaranteed rights and civil liberties not enjoyed by Chinese on the mainland, including the right of free speech and the right to assemble peaceably. In contrast to the mainland, where the judicial system is completely controlled by the Chinese Communist Party, Hong Kong would retain independent courts.

Despite such assurances, many Hong Kong residents emigrated from the island before sovereignty was officially transferred to China on June 30, 1997. Many have emigrated since then. Periodic attempts by Beijing to exert more influence in Hong Kong have triggered demonstrations and unrest there.

The Chinese government in Beijing has promised Taiwan the same "One Country, Two Systems" plan if it would agree to rejoin mainland China, but the Taiwanese government has expressed no interest in acting on this offer.

Lack of Religious Freedom

The People's Republic of China, like other Communist countries, actively discourages its citizens from practicing their religious beliefs. During the Cultural Revolution, Buddhist ancestor-worship shrines were torn apart, and it was made explicitly clear to religious missionaries that they were unwelcome. But for the most part, while persecution of Tibetan Buddhists and some Christian groups continued, the Chinese government's policy toward religious organizations became less oppressive during the 1970s and 1980s. That attitude changed in the 1990s with the growth of a faith known as Falun Gong.

A public movement in China since 1992, Falun Gong bases its spiritual practice on physical movement to traditional Chinese music and shares some concepts with Taoism, Buddhism, and traditional Chinese thought about the body and medicine. The Chinese government claims that the religion's beliefs about medicine are harmful and socially destabilizing. Falun Gong was labeled a cult by the Chinese government and its practice has been outlawed since 1999. During the 1990s and the early years of the 21st century, the Chinese government imprisoned more than 100,000 practitioners of Falun Gong and sent tens of thousands of others to labor camps without trial.

Practitioners of Falun Gong meditate in a park in New York City. A public spiritual movement since 1992, Falun Gong was outlawed in China in 1999 and has faced persecution by the authorities for over two decades. Thousands of members of the group have served sentences in prisons and labor camps for practicing the faith.

The Universal Declaration of Human Rights, which China signed along with other members of the United Nations, guarantees basic human rights such as freedom of speech and freedom of belief. However, the People's Republic of China maintains that it has the right to safeguard the stability of its government against movements it considers destructive like Falun Gong. Practitioners and supporters of the faith believe that freedom of religion is an important human right. They, like Tibetan Buddhists and Chinese Christians, have demonstrated that the search for religious freedom is a motivating factor behind emigration from China.

Text-Dependent Questions

1. Name the general who led the Nationalist forces against the Communists.
2. What happened on October 1, 1949?
3. What was the Great Leap Forward? What tragic results did it produce?

Research Project

Using library resources or the Internet, find out more about the Cultural Revolution. If possible, read first-person accounts of Chinese people who lived through that turbulent period. List the five most surprising things you learned.

3 COMING TO AMERICA

Many Chinese have found that the desires for political, personal, and religious freedom, as well as greater economic opportunities, are powerful incentives to immigrate to the United States and Canada. Although there have been periods of openness in Chinese immigration to North America, the Chinese have also faced major restrictions, particularly in the late 19th and early 20th centuries.

Chinese Immigration to the United States

The California gold rush, which began in 1848, triggered the first large wave of Chinese immigrants to North America. At first, the Chinese migrants prospected for gold alongside their American counterparts. By the mid-1850s, however, the gold mines had largely been played out, and Chinese settled in cities, particularly San Francisco.

Thousands of Chinese laborers were hired to help build the Transcontinental Railroad, begun in 1863. By the time the railroad was completed in 1869, Chinese made up about three-quarters of the workforce laying the western end of the line. The work was backbreaking and dangerous, and it's estimated that 1,200 to 1,500 Chinese laborers lost their lives on the project.

◀ Two groups of Chinese-American senior citizens enjoy card games on a sunny afernoon in Manhattan's Columbus Park, near New York's Chinatown neighborhood.

Early Chinese immigrants to North America were mostly from the southeastern province of Guangdong, although the provinces of Fujian, Zhejiang, and Hainan also sent significant numbers of immigrants, a great majority of whom were male.

While male Chinese laborers were encouraged to migrate, in general government officials from China and the United States (as well as Canada) discouraged Chinese families from settling in North America. China wanted to ensure its economy continued to benefit from goods and capital being sent back from North America. And American and Canadian officials wanted to keep the cheap labor working on railroads and in gold mines, while deterring an ethnic group many looked down on from completely assimilating into American society and threatening the status quo.

Those Chinese workers allowed into the United States made great sacrifices. The hours were long and hard, and they suffered from discrimination, which sometimes took the form of violence. In *Strangers from a Different Shore: A History of Asian Americans*, Ronald Takaki listed typical expressions from an English-Chinese phrase book published in 1875. Some of them—"He took it from me by violence" and "He cheated me out of my wages"—reflect the harsh experiences of the Chinese immigrant during that period.

From the 1850s on, some Californians sought to stop

Words to Understand in This Chapter

asylum—protection granted by a nation to someone who has left his or her native country as a political refugee.
entrepreneur—a person who takes on the financial risks of organizing and operating a business.
lawful permanent resident status—legal authorization to live and work in the United States indefinitely, and potentially to become a naturalized citizen.
veto—to exercise the executive power of rejecting a bill passed by the legislature; an instance of rejecting a bill.

> ### Documenting China's Human Rights Abuses
>
> Born in China in 1937, Harry Hongda Wu came of age while Chairman Mao was implementing his Great Leap Forward programs. In the 1960s, Wu was condemned as a "rightist," and for 19 years was forced to take on backbreaking work in labor camps located throughout the country.
>
> After escaping from China in 1985, Wu moved to the United States. There he gained American citizenship, wrote a revealing autobiography about his prison experience, *Bitter Winds*, and began speaking out about the practices of China's labor camps and other human rights abuses committed by the Chinese government. In his publications, Wu claims that some of the goods exported by China are products of forced labor. During the 1990s, Wu secretly traveled to China, where he continued to gather information on various abuses.
>
> During one such trip in 1995, Wu was caught by the Chinese government and arrested. Although he was convicted of spying for the American government and sentenced to prison, the Chinese government ultimately returned him to the United States in the interests of maintaining positive diplomatic relations. Wu tried to go back to China in March 2002, but authorities in Hong Kong refused to let him enter the country. He then resumed his life in the United States, where he continues to be a prominent advocate for democracy and human rights in China.

Chinese immigration. An 1858 California law would have prevented Chinese from entering the Golden State, but it was struck down as unconstitutional.

Eventually, the United States Congress took up the issue of Chinese immigration. In 1879, Congress passed a bill to prohibit Chinese from entering the country, but President Rutherford B. Hayes vetoed it. An 1882 bill, the Chinese Exclusion Act, was signed into law by President Chester A. Arthur.

With very narrow exceptions, the Chinese Exclusion Act forbade any person from China to enter the United States. Chinese who were already in the country were denied the possibility of becoming naturalized U.S. citizens. The Chinese Exclusion Act was set to expire in 10 years, but it was reauthorized for another decade in 1892 and reauthorized without any end date in 1902.

The act was finally repealed in 1943, in the midst of World War II. At that time, the United States and China were fighting a common enemy, Japan. And many Americans not only sympathized with the plight of people in China, but also came to see Chinese Americans in a different light.

Takaki reports that approximately 22 percent of all military-age Chinese American males served in the U.S. armed forces during the Second World War. Many other Chinese—male and female—worked in defense industries. Because there were no designated Chinese American units of the military, the Chinese were integrated into white units. Many American soldiers with European ethnic backgrounds, at first uncomfortable being integrated with minorities, learned to respect Chinese American soldiers as they fought as comrades in arms.

Immigration to the United States from the People's Republic of China was quite limited from the 1950s through the 1970s, a period during which the two countries didn't have full diplomatic relations (full relations were restored in 1979). On average, only about 1,350 people from the PRC were granted lawful permanent resident status in the United States each year during that three-decade period.

U.S. law also significantly limited the overall number of Asians eligible to immigrate—meaning there were few Chinese immigrants from Hong Kong or Taiwan—until the passage of

Upon signing into law the Immigration Act of 1965, President Lyndon B. Johnson declared that the national-origin quota system would "never again shadow the gate to the American nation with the twin barriers of prejudice and privilege."

52   Chinese Immigrants

President George W. Bush, flanked by members of Congress, signs the Enhanced Border Security and Visa Entry Reform Act, May 14, 2002. The legislation, passed in response to the September 11, 2001, terrorist attacks on the United States, tightened rules on the granting of visas.

the Immigration and Nationality Act of 1965. Afterward, immigration from Hong Kong and Taiwan increased dramatically. In total, the United States welcomed more than a quarter million lawful immigrants from Hong Kong, and more than 200,000 from Taiwan, during the 1970s and 1980s. Throughout the 1990s, both Hong Kong and Taiwan continued to send immigrants to the United States at a rate of well over 10,000 per year. By then, however, more people were immigrating to the United States from the People's Republic of China than from Hong Kong and Taiwan combined.

In the 21st century, the vast majority of Chinese immigrants to the United States have come from the mainland. In 2013, for example, more than 68,000 people from the mainland of the PRC were granted lawful permanent resident status in the United States. By comparison, only about 2,600 legal immigrants came from Hong Kong, and about 5,300 hailed from Taiwan.

Many Chinese immigrants are highly trained professionals or students who, after obtaining degrees from American universities, decide they want to remain in the United States (during the

2014–2015 academic year, more than 300,000 Chinese were enrolled in U.S. institutions of higher learning).

The Chinese government began permitting citizens to study abroad in the late 1970s. It recognized that China's population was woefully lacking in the kind of expertise necessary to build a modern economy and that China's universities—especially after the Cultural Revolution—were incapable of instilling that expertise. The government hoped that, after obtaining advanced degrees at foreign institutions, Chinese would return home and share their knowledge, whether as university professors or as business professionals. But most Chinese who have been educated abroad have stayed abroad. According to China's Ministry of Education, only a third of those who study overseas (whether in the United States or elsewhere) return to China; independent estimates put the actual proportion considerably lower.

To combat this "brain drain," China's government has been offering major financial incentives for experts to join the faculties of Chinese universities. This effort, however, has met with

A Chinese man (left) is sworn in as a U.S. citizen during a mass ceremony in New York City. Since the passing of the Immigration and Nationality Act of 1965 and other acts opening up immigration, many more Chinese newcomers have entered the country and have gone on to receive their U.S. citizenship.

limited success.

Chinese Immigration to Canada

After the United States barred Chinese workers from settling in the country, Canada encouraged the immigration of Chinese laborers to assist in the building of Canadian railways. Responding to the racial views of the time, the Canadian Parliament began charging a "head tax" for Chinese and South Asian (Indian) immigrants in 1885. The fee of $50—later raised to $500—was well beyond the means of laborers making one or two dollars a day. Later, the government sought additional ways to prohibit Asians from entering the country. For example, it decided to require a "continuous journey," meaning that immigrants to Canada had to travel from their country on a boat that made an uninterrupted passage. For immigrants or asylum seekers from Asia this was nearly impossible.

After World War II, Canadian immigration policy dictated that the Chinese share the same immigrant category—"of Asiatic origin"—with the Japanese. This meant that although China had been an ally of Canada during the war, the Chinese were restricted from immigrating to Canada. Some Canadian politicians were opposed to admitting more "Asiatics" into the country, even those who were relatives of Canadian citizens. The Canadian Citizenship Act of 1947 allowed the wives and children of citizens and legal residents of Canada to enter the country, but there was a specific clause that excluded "immigrants of any Asiatic race" from this provision.

Many Canadian Chinese, especially members of the Chinese Benevolent Association of Canada, lobbied to change such immigration laws, but the gap between the number of Chinese people and the number of other immigrants allowed to enter the country only widened. It was not until 1967 that Canadian legislators finally lifted restrictions based on nationality, ethnic group, class, or area of origin.

Anthony Chan, an expert on Chinese immigration to Canada, observed in his book *Gold Mountain* that throughout

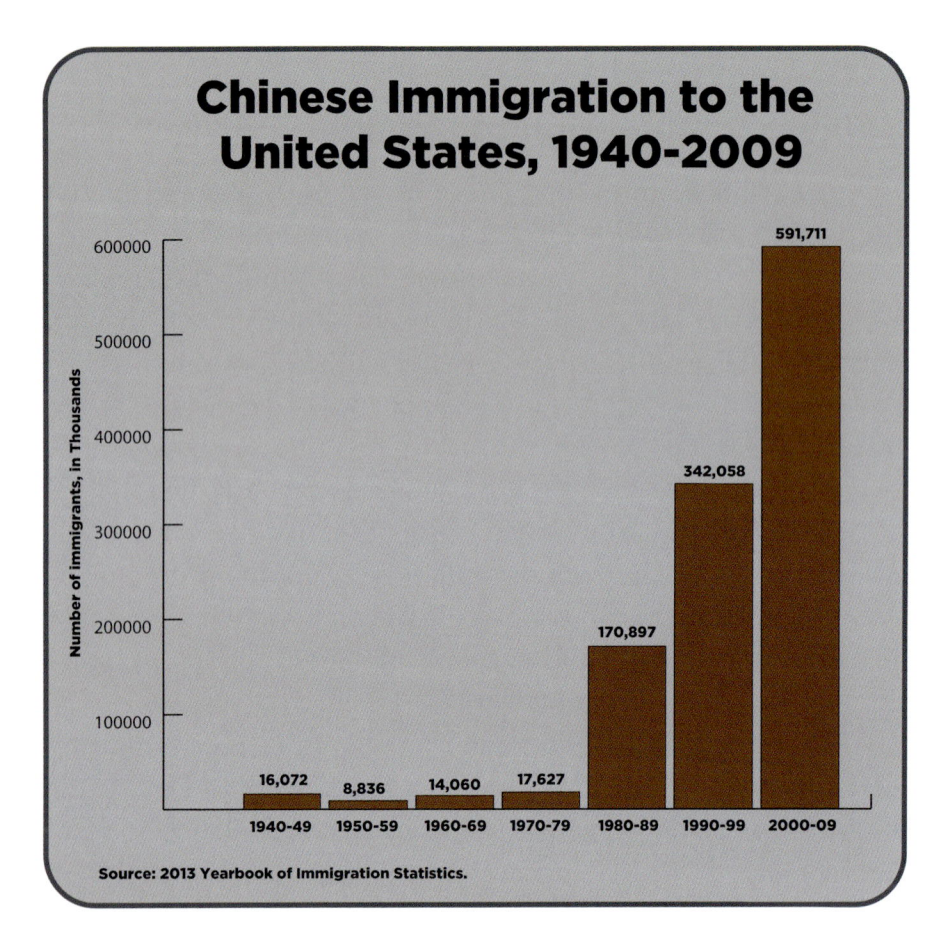

Chinese Immigration to the United States, 1940-2009

Decade	Number of immigrants
1940-49	16,072
1950-59	8,836
1960-69	14,060
1970-79	17,627
1980-89	170,897
1990-99	342,058
2000-09	591,711

Source: 2013 Yearbook of Immigration Statistics.

the history of early Chinese immigration, many newcomers felt ties to the general continent of North America rather than to the individual nations of Canada or the United States. Chan wrote:

> [A] Vancouver cannery worker writing to his peasant family in Taishan would not refer to Canada but to Gold Mountain, just as another family in the same district might hear from their relatives in San Francisco who would talk of Gold Mountain but not about *Meiguo* (America).
>
> Racist attitudes of the white population helped crystallize Chinese North America into a cohesive community, but perhaps the strongest glue was the community's passionate interest in the affairs and politics of China.

U.S.–China Relations

Of particular concern for Chinese immigrants was the issue of how China's political system could continue to make immigration difficult for friends and family still living in the homeland. So much depended on the state of diplomatic relations between the North American countries and China. Canada did not recognize the Communist government in Beijing as legitimate until the early 1970s, while the United States only recognized the British possession of Hong Kong and the Nationalist government in Taiwan for most of the 1960s and 1970s. As a result, anyone who wanted to legally immigrate from the People's Republic of China to the United States had to first get to Taiwan or Hong Kong.

Full diplomatic relations between the United States and Communist China were finally established in 1979, and three years later, the People's Republic of China was permitted to send

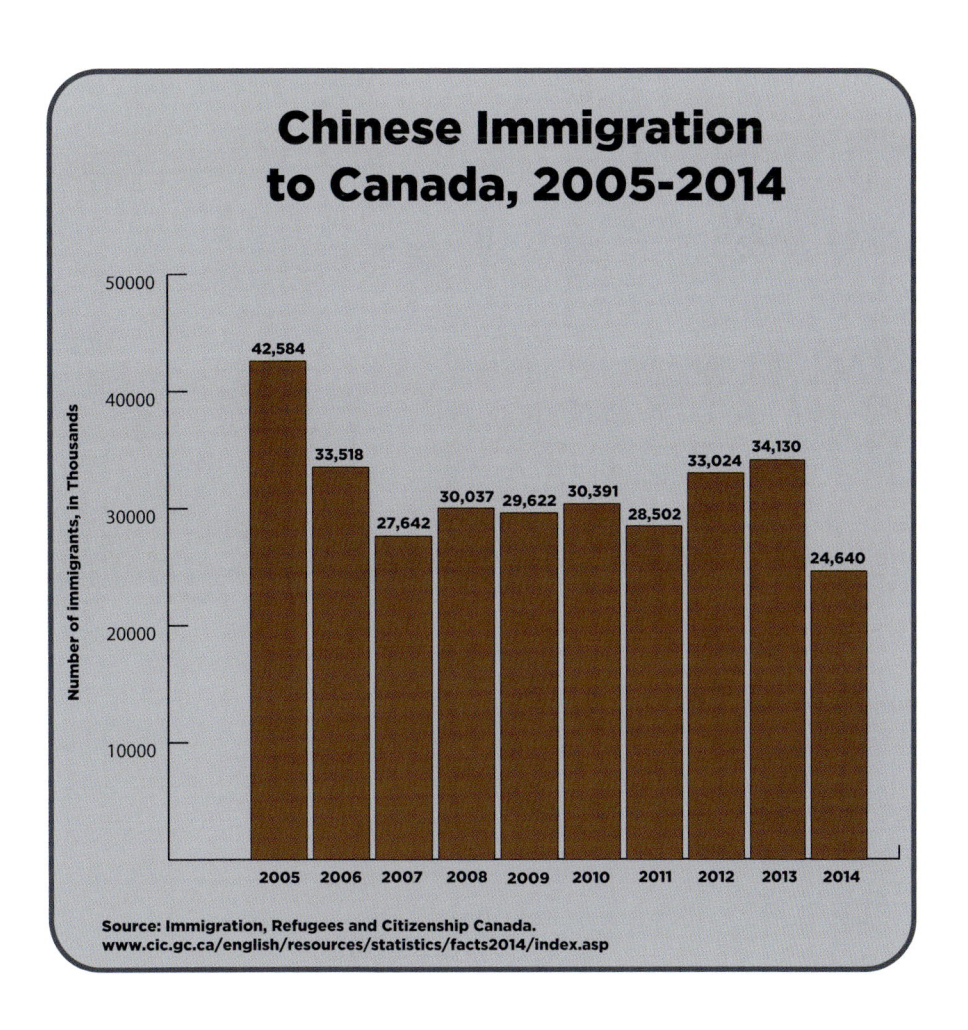

Chinese Immigration to Canada, 2005-2014

Year	Number of immigrants
2005	42,584
2006	33,518
2007	27,642
2008	30,037
2009	29,622
2010	30,391
2011	28,502
2012	33,024
2013	34,130
2014	24,640

Source: Immigration, Refugees and Citizenship Canada.
www.cic.gc.ca/english/resources/statistics/facts2014/index.asp

Many Chinese professionals, especially those in the medical field, have found that their credentials are not transferable in the U.S. and have thus had to take employment with fewer skill requirements.

immigrants to the United States, under the conditions of the 20,000-per-country limit that applied to other Eastern Hemisphere countries. In recognition of the new diplomatic relations between the United States and China, the U.S. government pledged it would not interfere in the affairs between China and Taiwan, although Taiwan was given a separate immigration quota by special amendment.

Although the United States had established diplomatic relations with the People's Republic of China, the U.S. government remained concerned about China's ongoing human rights violations. The events in Tiananmen Square in 1989 prompted the administration of President George H. W. Bush to allow Chinese citizens who had entered the United States before the massacre to remain in the country. This action benefited Chinese students, tourists, and people with temporary work visas. The Chinese Student Adjustment Act of 1992 helped many of these individuals become permanent residents and, if they wanted, U.S. citizens.

Those who could not legally leave China found other ways to emigrate. The 1990s saw growing numbers of undocumented Chinese immigrants leave the country. Those who were caught were usually deported back to China.

Text-Dependent Questions

1. What event triggered the first major wave of Chinese immigration to the United States?
2. Name the U.S. law that barred Chinese immigrants from entering the country. When did the law go into effect? When was it repealed?
3. What steps did the Canadian government take to limit Chinese immigration before the 1960s?

Research Project

Investigate the contribution of Chinese laborers to the construction of the Transcontinental Railroad. Write a two-page report.

4 From Chinatown to the Suburbs

Chinese immigrants tend to settle in the same regions of the United States and Canada, a pattern that has resulted in the creation of large Chinese neighborhoods. Many major North American cities, as well as smaller cities and suburbs, now have well-established Chinese communities.

Chinese American and Chinese Canadian Enclaves

The Pacific coastal cities—Los Angeles and San Francisco, California; Seattle, Washington; and Vancouver, British Columbia—have long appealed to Chinese immigrants for their proximity to the homeland. Chinese American communities developed in these cities long ago, in the days when Chinese immigrants arrived on the West Coast by way of a ship journey across the Pacific Ocean. Today more than half of the Chinese in the United States live in the Pacific states. A large segment also lives in Hawaii, which since the second half of the 19th century has had a particularly high Asian population. Hawaii's communities include many Chinese Americans and Americans of mixed ethnicity.

Although the earliest Chinese immigrants made their homes in the West, many others eventually settled in regions across the

◂The streets of Chinatown neighborhoods often come alive as bustling marketplaces. Many Chinese immigrants choose to settle in Chinatown neighborhoods, which are found in many major cities of North America, including San Francisco, New York, Philadelphia, and Toronto.

United States. A large number of Chinese immigrants live on the East Coast (particularly in New York, New Jersey, and Massachusetts) and in the Midwest (Illinois, Michigan, and Ohio). The majority have settled in cultural enclaves, typically called Chinatown, located within or just outside the major cities.

Chinatowns consist primarily of housing and businesses that serve the Chinese community. Such enterprises typically include Chinese restaurants and teahouses, jewelry stores, beauty salons, retail stores, open-air markets, professional offices, and garment manufacturers. Often popular with tourists, Chinatowns also cater to members of other ethnic groups who want a taste of Chinese food and culture. These enclaves also are especially important as entry points for many Chinese newcomers, who find the transition to life in the United States or Canada easier to handle among people who speak their language.

New York City contains the largest Chinese population outside Asia. During the second half of the 20th century, the city's Chinese population exploded, growing from about 33,000 in 1960, to around 240,000 in 1990, to more than 360,000 in 2000. In 2010, according to data from the U.S. Census Bureau, more than 486,000 ethnic Chinese were living in New York City, making the Chinese by far the most numerous Asian group there. Cantonese is widely spoken in New York, as a large portion of the city's Chinese community has origins in South China.

New York actually features two major Chinatowns—one that is squeezed into a two-square-mile (5.2-sq-km) area of the lower East Side of the Manhattan borough, and the other locat-

Words to Understand in This Chapter

benevolent organization—an organization that serves a charitable (as opposed to profit-making) purpose.
tong—a Chinese association or club that is often associated with organized crime.
tongxianghui—a Chinese association of people who come from the same native place.

A woman browses a street-side seafood market store in Brooklyn's Eighth Avenue Chinatown

ed in Flushing, Queens, where large numbers of Taiwanese immigrants began congregating in the 1970s. These Mandarin-speaking Chinese sometimes refer to the region as "Little Taipei," after the capital city of Taiwan.

Other popular Chinatown districts can be found in the cities of San Francisco, Chicago, Boston, Philadelphia, Houston, Vancouver, and Toronto. As increased Chinese immigration has attracted more and more newcomers, the borders of most major metropolitan Chinatowns have expanded, and Chinese communities have naturally spilled outside the boundaries of Chinatowns and into suburban enclaves.

A sense of community is very important to the Chinese people, so the Chinatowns and similar neighborhoods have served to put new immigrants in familiar situations, with institutions they already know and trust. Many Chinese immigrants have relied upon the Chinatown social networks for assistance in beginning their new lives.

From Chinatown to the Suburbs 63

Business Owners and Professional Workers

Chinese Americans are renowned for their skills in starting up and running successful small businesses. Many immigrants become entrepreneurs, organizing and managing their own businesses. These may be small stores, restaurants, or service businesses such as dry cleaners or laundries.

For the early Chinese immigrants to North America, racial discrimination was a crucial factor behind job availability.

> ### "Chinese" v. "Asian American" or "Asianadian"
>
> Recent immigrants have trouble understanding how an ethnic Chinese person can identify himself or herself simply as Asian American or Asianadian (Asian Canadian). After all, Chinese people generally distinguish themselves from the Japanese, Koreans, and other Asian ethnic groups, each of which has its own distinct language and culture. However, in North America many Chinese, Japanese, Vietnamese, and other Asian groups often find that they have been lumped together as one ethnic entity and treated similarly. Some Asians have taken something positive from this generalization, as it has forced them to acknowledge the political concerns that they have in common.
>
> One issue over which Asian groups have come together is hate crimes. Statistically, Asians aren't likely to be the targets of racially or ethnically motivated violence--in 2013, according to data from the FBI's Unified Crime Reports, Asians accounted for just 3 percent of hate-crime victims in the United States. Still, no level of hate-crime victimization is acceptable.
>
> One famous hate-crime incident occurred on June 19, 1982, when a Chinese American man named Vincent Chin was murdered in Detroit, Michigan. Two white unemployed autoworkers, who blamed the then-booming Japanese auto industry for the loss of their jobs, mistakenly identified Chin as Japanese. While uttering ethnic slurs, they cornered him in an alley and savagely beat him to death. In a plea bargain, the two men received a punishment of three years' probation and a fine of $3,780.
>
> This sentence outraged many in the Chinese American community, and they rallied to protest. Many other Asian ethnic groups joined them. In a rare instance of solidarity, some Chinese Americans acknowledged their commonality with Japanese Americans and Korean Americans. The idea of Asian Americans working together on issues gained more credence as a result of Vincent Chin's tragic death.
>
> Seven years later, when a young Chinese American named Ming Hai "Jim" Loo was killed by racists who mistakenly thought he was Vietnamese, members of the Asian American communities were prepared. They were organized, well funded, and ready to protest to make sure that others didn't suffer the same injustice that Vincent Chin's family encountered years before. Loo's killers received long prison sentences.

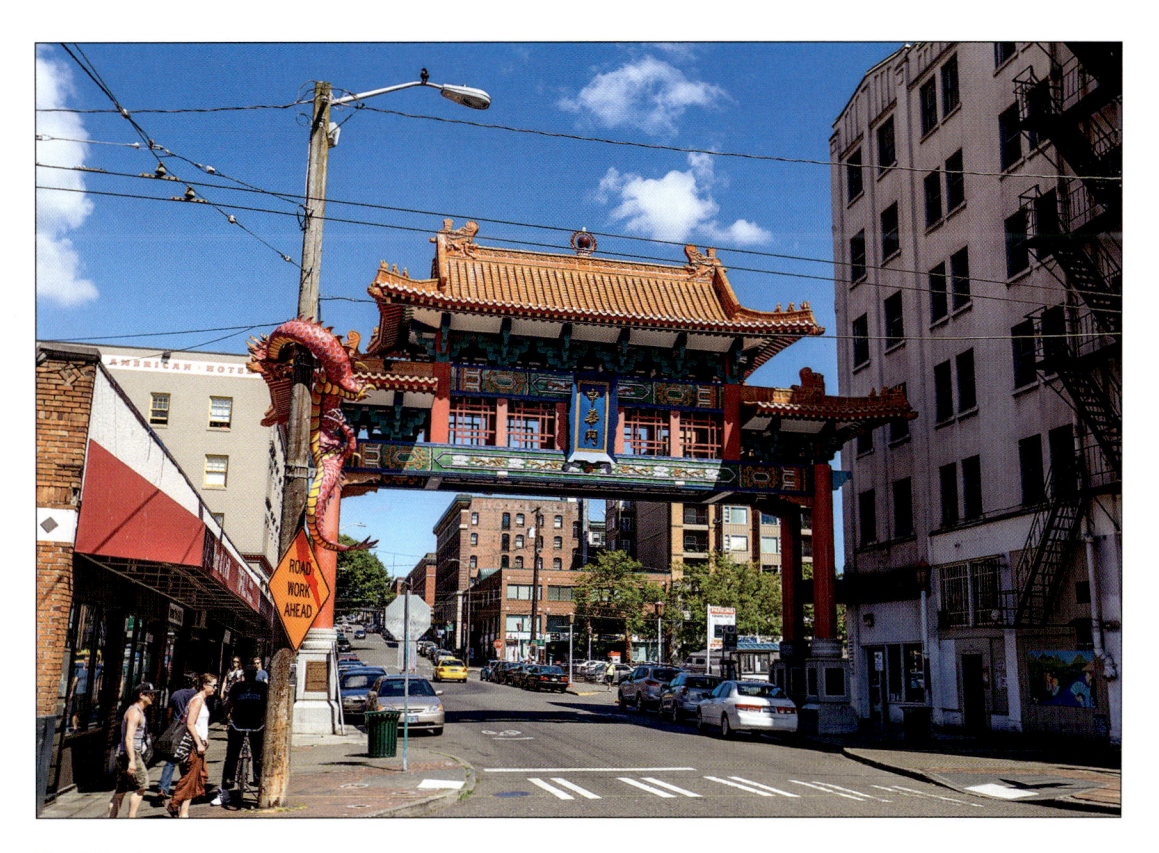

The Chinatown neighborhood in Seattle encompasses the blocks east of Fifth Avenue in the downtown part of the city.

Because Chinese were prohibited from becoming citizens, owning land, voting, or holding public office during the early 20th century, many were excluded from major areas of employment in the general economy. In the established white communities, a large number of Chinese found work by opening their own laundries and restaurant businesses.

Even for those with college degrees, employment opportunities were very limited. In the 1940s, a Stanford University report observed that it was almost impossible during that time to place a Chinese or Japanese graduate in a position, whether in engineering, manufacturing, or business. Chinese Americans with bachelor's degrees and even advanced degrees and who spoke excellent English sometimes found themselves working as servants just so they could feed their families.

Today, it is fairly typical for Chinese newcomers to work in a handful of industries that are friendly toward speakers of

Chinese dialects. These industries include restaurants, Chinese or other Asian import stores, and the garment trade (notably clothing manufacture). Educated Chinese immigrants can also find employment in many other fields, including engineering, investment, architecture, insurance, law, and fashion design and entertainment. They have been accepted in many more fields in recent years than they were from the 1930s to the 1950s, with higher-paying occupations available to them. However, it is sometimes necessary for medical professionals trained in China to take other jobs while they undergo the certification process to practice in the United States.

The skills that Chinese immigrants hold before their journey to North America have a significant impact on the kind of work they end up doing in their new country. Those who were educated in technical fields or who speak English well can frequently obtain white-collar, professional jobs and can more easily assimilate into mainstream American culture.

Because the average wage level in the United States and Canada is so much higher than in China, many immigrants are attracted primarily by the promise of higher income.

Better Pay in America

In spite of China's recent progress, wages in the United States tend to be much higher than those in China, even for unskilled jobs. When asked by immigration expert Marlowe Hood why he had come to America, Chen Yuan, a Chinese immigrant from the city of Fuzhou, replied:

> When the income differential between China and the United States is 1:2 rather than 1:15 or 1:20, that is when Fuzhounese will stop going and even start to come back. . . . Look at it this way—in terms of income potential for the average worker, one year [of work] in the United States equals 15 Chinese years.

Chinese immigration researcher Ko-Lin Chin made a similar discovery when he studied a group of 300 undocumented Fujianese immigrants. In his book *Smuggled Chinese: Clandestine Immigration to the United States*, he reported his survey results: "About 61 percent of my respondents said they came to the United States for only one reason—to make money. Another 25 percent stated that their primary motive was to make money but also mentioned one or more non-monetary reasons for coming."

In 2010, according to the World Bank, more than 11 percent of China's population lived on less than $2 per day. Coming from such extreme poverty, Chinese immigrants may find the prospect of even a minimum-wage job in the United States extremely appealing. Even wealthy immigrants who have moved from China's cities find the wages and standard of living in North America to be much higher than that of China.

On the whole, Chinese Americans have enjoyed remarkable prosperity. Using 2010 data from the U.S. Census Bureau, the Pew Research Center calculated median household income for Chinese Americans at $65,050. By comparison, median household income for the U.S. population overall was $49,800. Much of the success of Chinese Americans can be attributed to high levels of educational attainment.

Problems Facing Immigrant Laborers

Many recent Chinese immigrants have arrived in America in debt. In order to pay back passage fees from China, as well as to afford day-to-day living expenses, they have to work constantly, often finding little time for their families. Some Chinese immigrants find jobs in Chinatown garment factories making less than minimum wage. They are typically paid per piece of work rather than at an hourly rate. In her book *Chinatown: A Portrait of a Closed Society*, Gwen Kinkead reported:

> In the four Chinatown shops I visited, everyone put in at least sixty hours a week, some for less than $200. A handful earned over $300. The majority made about $4 an hour, slightly less than burger flippers in McDonald's working nine to five at minimum wage—$4.25 an hour [at the time]. . . . When the piece rates drop below union minimums, or minimum wage, workers silently knuckle under and try to recover the lost wages by working even longer hours.

Many Chinese immigrant women who do not speak English find work as seamstresses in the garment industry. A study of garment workers in San Francisco's Chinatown found that 72 percent of the workers were women whose husbands were also working but in other fields, mostly in the restaurant business.

The differences between the employment of Chinese American men and women are not surprising, considering the employment standards of China. While the Communist government officially considers men and women to be equal, traditional Chinese families often value sons more than daughters and treat women with less respect. In general the responsibility for most of the housework and family care still falls upon women. The attitudes of Chinese women toward the American ideal of gender equality are greatly influenced by their education and where they live.

Generational Concerns

Sometimes the U.S.- or Canadian-born children of Chinese immigrants must help run the household or assist their parents in various other ways because their parents have limited English skills. This situation in which children are in the position of family responsibility runs counter to Chinese custom, in which the elder members have near-complete authority. Such change in the family structure often causes great stress for older immigrants.

Some children face a different challenge: they have difficulty acclimating to life in their new homeland because they immigrated many years after their parents. Such children may have spent years in China or Taiwan, where they were raised by grandparents until their parents could afford to send for them. In her book *Teenage Refugees from China Speak Out*, Colleen She interviewed Yi-Hua, a young girl who came to the United States from Beijing long after her parents' arrival:

> My immigration here was planned by my parents. I have been separated from them for nearly ten years. It is difficult to come to a strange land and live with parents you did not grow up with. I feel that getting reacquainted with my parents will be my greatest challenge.

Transitions for children like Yi-Hua can be especially difficult. Not only have they been deprived of those months and years with their parents, but they also are challenged to form new relationships both within and outside the family in their strange new country.

Chinese American Organizations

Chinese immigrants can turn to various groups for help and guidance in acclimating to their new culture. These include family associations, or social service groups such as the Chinese-American Planning Council, which evolved in the late 1960s and 1970s. Services offered by the organization include job training, legal advice, health care, day care, and translation. Family associations also provide care for elders and those in distress.

Unlike many European American immigrants who turn to Christian churches or Jewish synagogues for assistance in settling into their new homeland, Chinese immigrants typically do not depend on religious institutions for support. After decades of Communist rule, some are not religious at all, and those who are tend to worship in the home, usually through ancestor worship

Many Chinese Americans are finding success today as white-collar professionals and small business owners. Immigrants of past generations did not have the same financial success, often because they were denied the basic rights enjoyed by U.S. citizens and thus excluded from many job fields.

(meditation or paying respects to deceased family members). There is, however, a minority population of Chinese immigrant Christians. They often participate in activities provided by Chinese churches in the United States, such as youth fellowship clubs, women's guilds, and education and English classes for new immigrants.

Another well-established Chinese group that helps new immigrants is the Chinese Six Companies. The organization evolved from early immigrant groups called *huiguan*, the Cantonese word for "meeting hall." Years ago, Chinese people would gather together in meeting halls to provide each other with mutual support and help in their personal lives as well as in their businesses. Gradually, these social organizations came to be called "companies." Over the years the many companies consolidated and in 1862 became the Chinese Consolidated Benevolent Association, more commonly known as the Chinese Six Companies. This association helps new immigrants find employment and housing, and also provides social opportunities for its members. The organization has also been known to give business loans and help members who have fallen into debt.

Another community support group for the Chinese is the *tongxianghui* (native-place organization). This kind of social network, which first existed in China, welcomes people who are related and/or come from the same place. For much of Chinese American history, most place-based associations were Cantonese and were comprised of people from the Guangdong Province, located in southeast China. Members of the Cantonese *tongxianghui* in America typically allied themselves with China's Nationalist movement during the first half of the 20th century. As anti-Communists, they strongly supported the Nationalist government in Taiwan.

Beginning in the 1990s, immigrants from China—both legal and undocumented—formed their own community associations, such as the United Chinese Associations of New York, the Fukien American Association, the United Fujianese American Association, and the American Fujian Association of Commerce and Industry. Unlike earlier organizations, which were fiercely anti-Communist, many of the newer associations were officially pro-Communist.

Yet another kind of Chinese association is the family-name organization, made up of members with the same last name. Some groups combine with others to form larger organizations. For example, the Four Brothers Association is a multifamily benevolent organization that for a small yearly fee grants membership to anyone with the name Quan or one of the group's three other surnames. The association provides free dinners for members, burials for members without family, and other services.

Tongs are groups that were originally formed as benevolent protective associations to help protect the interests of the Chinese community, particularly in dealing with unfair and discriminatory laws. Although some tongs today are legitimate associations, others have been known to be associated with organized crime, even if not all their members are criminals. Some law-abiding Chinese join tongs for a variety of reasons, such as for protection or to obtain payments for debts.

One of the largest associations in New York's Chinatown is the Chinese Consolidated Benevolent Association (CCBA), which runs schools and fosters programs to preserve Chinese culture. A politically conservative and somewhat self-protective organization, the CCBA focuses mostly on supporting Taiwan in its political struggle against the People's Republic of China.

Membership in Chinese American associations such as the CCBA provides new immigrants with a support system that guides their entry into the established community. However, membership in such groups does not always ensure harmony. Some American-born Chinese (nicknamed "ABCs") may believe they have little in common with recent immigrants, who are sometimes derogatively referred to as "fresh off the boat," or "FOBs."

Preserving Chinese Heritage and Identity

Since the mid-1970s many Chinese Americans and Chinese Canadians have become interested in the cultural history of earlier generations. Some Chinese living in North America have formed or joined groups that work to preserve accounts of their past.

Formed in 1981, the Chinese Canadian National Council (originally the Chinese Canadian National Council for Equality), or CCNC, sponsors activities that are mainly apolitical. The organization focuses on maintaining the historical and cultural aspects of the Chinese Canadian community. Specifically, it gathers historical artifacts, organizes an annual heritage exhibition and festival, sponsors a scholarship fund in Chinese Canadian studies, and promotes cooperation among various ethnic, cultural, and civil liberties associations. By furthering education about Chinese Canadians, the CCNC hopes to increase awareness and understanding of the unique contributions that Chinese Canadians have made to the larger society. In the United States, groups like the Chinese Historical Society of America and the Chinese Culture Foundation pursue a similar agenda.

Text-Dependent Questions

1. Which American city is home to the largest ethnic Chinese community outside of Asia?
2. What is the general name for a Chinese enclave in a North American city?
3. Why do older Chinese immigrants sometimes have difficulty accepting help from their American- or Canadian-born children?

Research Project

If your family is Chinese and you speak a Chinese language, write a few sentences in that language and translate them into English. If you're not Chinese, use the Internet to learn how to say four or five basic phrases (such as *hello, thank you*, and *goodbye*) in Mandarin or Cantonese.

5 BLENDING TRADITIONS

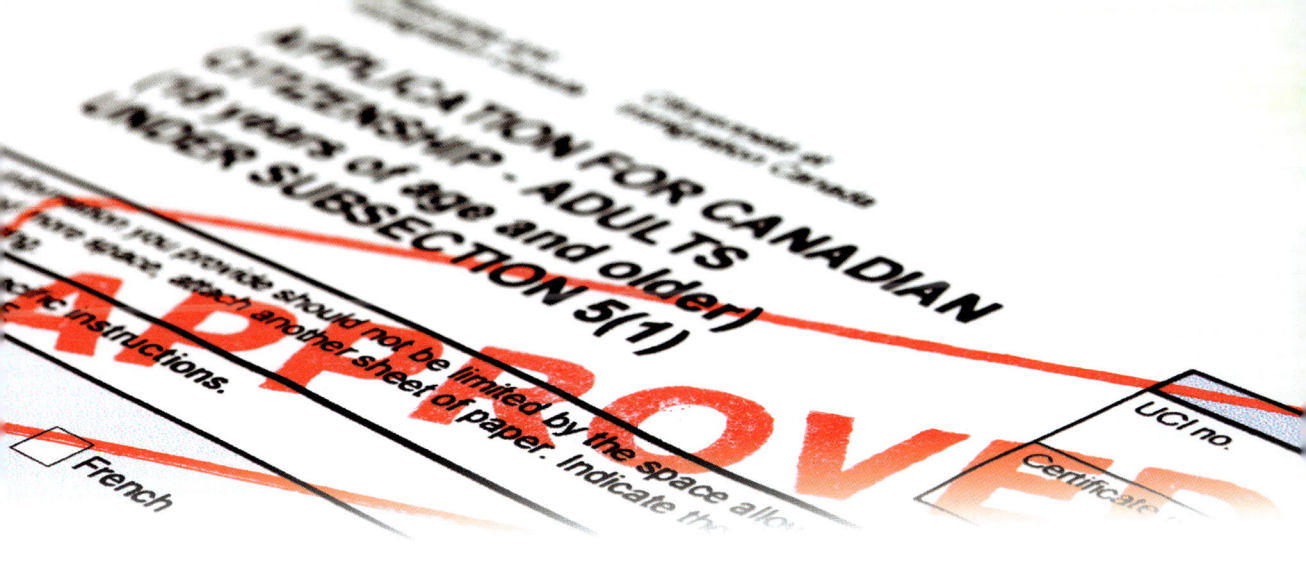

The degree to which Chinese assimilate into American or Canadian society varies widely. Some feel strongly about holding onto their Chinese culture and traditions. Others are willing to give up as many Chinese traits as possible to seem thoroughly North American. However, many—perhaps most—prefer to maintain some Chinese traditions while dropping others as they seek to assimilate.

Growing Up in America

Whether a person grows up in Chinese or American society will affect many aspects of his or her behavior, says a Chinese American interviewee who discussed his viewpoint in *Asian American Experiences in the United States* by Joann Faung Jean Lee. He believes that the Chinese person raised in China will differ significantly from the same person raised in Western society. Citing behavioral differences as an example, he explained to Lee that Asians raised in America tend to be more aggressive and less formal than Asians who grew up in Asia. He identifies other differences:

> Asian Americans dress the American way. Whereas Asian[s], regardless of how long they've been here, are basically Asian in look and dress. I don't know how to describe it, but there is

◀ A family of Chinese descent enjoys the festivities at an outdoor event in Vancouver, Canada.

some subtle difference, and I can tell. There is a difference in the way they comb their hair, their gestures and the types of clothes they wear. When I was in college, I had trouble getting accepted by Asian Americans. I also had trouble getting accepted by Chinese from Hong Kong. . . . It was not that they wouldn't accept me, but there was a barrier. . . . Since most of them came from Hong Kong, there was a common bond, and I became an outsider.

After years of living in North America, many Chinese Americans and Chinese Canadians develop their own culture, which consists of a blend of elements from both Chinese and Western cultures. This is particularly evident in the rituals and traditions of special occasions. Rather than dropping the traditions of their ancestors or slighting those of their new country, Chinese Americans and Chinese Canadians often use both.

Author Ben Fong-Torres provides an example of this blending of cultures in *The Rice Room: Growing Up Chinese-American from Number Two Son to Rock 'N' Roll.* In the book he remembers attending a Chinese American wedding that incorporated Western and Eastern elements. The bride and groom exchanged vows in a Western-style church, and they were carried out in English, but other rituals reflected many Eastern traditions. The wedding reception consisted of a lavish Chinese banquet. The traditional Chinese dishes were served: roast duck and shark fin soup, which according to tradition represent power and prosperity. The honored guests made toasts in both English and Chinese.

Words to Understand in This Chapter

equinox—either of two times during the year (falling around the first day of spring and the first day of autumn) when day and night are the same length.
intermarriage—marriage between two people of different races or religions.
ritual—a ceremony that is always performed the same way.

76 Chinese Immigrants

Children in traditional dress participate in a Chinese New Year parade in San Francisco.

Keeping the Chinese Heritage

Some Chinese families do not make complete assimilation into Western society their primary goal. Traditional Chinese families, fearing that their children and grandchildren will lose their heritage, may pressure them to marry only other ethnic Chinese. Researcher Betty Lee Sung, who studied the attitudes and experiences of the Chinese regarding intermarriage and integration, noted that in some cases those who did marry outside the Chinese community were not accepted by their families and Chinese friends—even after 30 to 40 years of marriage.

One Chinese immigrant who had to deal with others' disapproval of her interracial marriage was Sue Jean Lee Suettinger, who was interviewed for the book *Asian American Experiences in the United States*. When Suettinger, who came to the United States as a small child, chose to marry a man who was not Chinese, she encountered much negative pressure from her fam-

Blending Traditions

ily. In fact, during the six months leading to the wedding, her father refused to speak to her. It was only after the wedding that she made peace with her family, but in the interview she admitted there were consequences to marrying someone of a different ethnic background, one of which was that her children did not learn to speak Chinese. It is likely that Suettinger's children will want to learn more about China at some point. Second- and third-generation Chinese Americans often feel curious about the land of their ancestors, as do Americans from many different ethnic groups.

Author Maxine Hong Kingston, the daughter of a Chinese immigrant, discusses in her 1980 book *China Men* how she really wanted to see her parents' homeland, but was also concerned about the difficulties that such a visit might involve:

> I'd like to go to China if I can get a visa and—more difficult—permission from my family, who are afraid that applying for a visa would call attention to us: the relatives in China would get in trouble for having American capitalist connections, and we Americans would be put in relocation camps during the next witch hunt for Communists.

However, it should be noted that since U.S.–Chinese relations have improved it has become possible for many later-generation Americans to return to the country their parents or grandparents left. This group now has more freedom to visit distant relatives or merely see the sights.

Celebrating Holiday Traditions and Customs

Many Westerners are familiar with the Chinese New Year, also called the Spring Festival. Since traditional Chinese culture follows the lunar calendar, the Chinese New Year is celebrated on different dates of the Western calendar. It falls on the first day of the first month of the lunar year, which usually is anytime between late January and early February. The Chinese New Year celebrates the birth of spring and new beginnings, marking a time of renewed hope for a successful future. Considered the most important of Chinese American holidays, the New Year features celebrations that can last for a month.

> ## The Year of the Zodiac
>
> Like many other Asian groups, the Chinese use the lunar calendar, which bases its months on the changing phases of the moon. According to the Chinese Zodiac, each lunar year (consisting of twelve months) is represented by one of 12 animals, so that the Chinese New Year introduces the Year of the Rat, Ox, Tiger, Hare, Dragon, Snake, Horse, Sheep, Monkey, Rooster, Dog, or Pig. Some people believe that a person will have the characteristics of the animal representing the year in which he or she was born. For example, someone born in the Year of the Horse is said to be hardworking, honest, independent, and sociable.
>
> In 1993 the U.S. Postal Service began to honor the Chinese New Year with a series of Lunar New Year stamps. Designed by Clarence Lee, this commemorative series started with the Year of the Rooster (1993), and was then followed by the Year of the Dog (1994), Boar (1995), Rat (1996), Ox (1997), Tiger (1998), Hare (1999), Dragon (2000), Snake (2001), Horse (2002), Sheep (2003), and Monkey (2004). The Lunar New Year stamp project was first proposed by members of the Organization of Chinese Americans (OCA).

Before the New Year arrives, people thoroughly clean their homes, buy new clothes, and get haircuts so that they start off the year looking their best. Homes are decorated with good-luck poems written in Chinese characters and a pine bough money tree adorned with coins and paper flowers. Because the Chinese consider the color red to be extremely lucky, they often use it for decorations, particularly during the Chinese New Year.

On the day of the New Year, Chinese families gather together to share feasts and exchange gifts. As part of the celebration, older relatives give children a "lucky red envelope" containing money. Called "Hong Bao" in Chinese, the red color of this traditional gift is thought to contain positive power and thus bring good luck both to the giver and the receiver of the gift.

New Year is also a time to honor one's ancestors for some traditional Chinese families. They keep an altar in the home that features the names of the father's family members going back for several generations. During the New Year holiday, family members place food offerings on the altar, light incense, and bow in honor of their ancestors.

In addition to having ceremonies in the home, family-name

From Hong Kong to Hollywood

Many Americans are fans of kung fu movies, which feature the Chinese method of unarmed combat that uses hands, elbows, knees, or feet to strike blows. In the past, kung fu films were seldom viewed by a mass audience. Hong Kong martial arts star Jackie Chan helped to change that, establishing a successful action-comedy career with a following spanning two continents.

Born Chan Kong-Sang in 1954, just after his parents had fled to Hong Kong from the Shandong Province, Chan entered a family that was struggling with poverty. He has told interviewers that his parents were so poor that they almost asked the doctor who delivered Chan to adopt him.

At the age of six, Chan attended the Chinese Drama Academy. After growing up and becoming a working professional, he earned a reputation in the film business, first as a stuntman and then as an actor who did his own stunts. Like his predecessor, kung fu legend Bruce Lee, Jackie Chan eventually made the transition from Hong Kong star to American movie idol. In 2002 he received a star on the Hollywood Walk of Fame.

In his movies, Chan often addresses the culture clash between Westerners and Chinese, making Americans laugh while they reconsider their assumptions about Eastern cultures. Some of his movies also deal with popular Asian American themes and issues. For instance, the plot of his 1996 film *Rumble in the Bronx* involves a rivalry between tong bosses in New York's Chinatown.

---

groups and social associations also get together to celebrate the major festivals. In cities where these groups are large, they have been known to host big restaurant dinners for the Chinese New Year. The Chinatowns in major cities often bring in the New Year by hosting parades and setting off fireworks.

Chinese New Year parades usually feature the lion dance, a costumed performance that is thought to bring good fortune and joy to the spectators as well as the performers. The tradition of the lion dance started during the Han dynasty, about 2,000 years ago, and is similar to Taiwanese and Korean dances. Often mistaken by Westerners as a dragon costume, the lion costume requires just two dancers. (The dragon dance, which may also be performed at parades, involves more than two people.) One person dances as the head of the lion, controlling its facial expressions to indicate happiness or anger, while the other dances as the tail. Three musical performers, playing the drum, cymbals, and gong, accompany the dancers.

The Chinese New Year festivities last until the 15th day of the new lunar month, and end with the Lantern Festival. This holiday features lantern exhibits, lion and dragon dances, and the serving of boiled sweet rice dumplings called *tang yuan*.

Another important Chinese holiday is Qingming, which falls in early spring, often during the first part of April. Its name literally means "the clear and bright festival." On Qingming, Chinese families honor their dead ancestors. Traditional celebrations involve cleaning family gravesites or places set aside to remember family members. After the graves are cleaned, some people leave offerings of food and paper replicas of money to their ancestors. Other families celebrate in a less-solemn fashion by having picnics, flying kites, and decorating with flower garlands.

The Mid-Autumn Festival, which falls on the 15th day of the 8th lunar month (usually in September), is second only to the Chinese New Year in significance. Sometimes called the Autumn Moon Festival, the holiday marks the end of the summer harvest and is a time for giving thanks. The Mid-Autumn Festival occurs around the time of the autumnal equinox, when the moon appears to be at its largest and brightest.

Families celebrate the holiday by gathering together and holding feasts, which include an abundance of fruits and "moon cakes"—palm-sized round cakes traditionally made with a sweet bean-paste filling. In the center of the cake is a golden egg yoke that looks like a bright moon. Chinatowns often host Mid-Autumn Festivals featuring arts and crafts displays, food and drink booths, parades, and live entertainment by dancers, acrobats, and martial artists.

Although in China this holiday has a separate designated date for families to reunite and have large dinners, in the United

Musicians play traditional Chinese music at the annual Eldridge Street Festival in New York.

States and Canada such festivities occur more commonly during the Chinese New Year or during American holidays such as Thanksgiving, when most family members can get time off from work.

The date that Chinese immigrants celebrate China's national holiday varies depending on the ethnic makeup of the particular community. Every year, the Cantonese populations of Chinatowns celebrate on October 10, which is the national holiday of Taiwan's Nationalist government. The Cantonese do not acknowledge October 1, which is the Communist national holiday, although the Fujianese communities generally consider that day the proper time for celebrations. Many Chinese Americans and Chinese Canadians skip these two dates altogether and throw themselves wholeheartedly into celebrating the holidays of their adopted countries, such as Independence Day, Canada Day, or Thanksgiving.

Celebrations of certain American-style holidays have sometimes startled new immigrants, although most of them—especially the children—quickly learn to adapt. Ben Fong-Torres recalled his mother's first encounter with Halloween:

> Two months after her arrival in Oakland, my mother was home one evening when her doorbell rang. She pulled back the curtain on the front door window and found herself confronted by two children—one a ghost, the other a witch. Even though they were clearly children, they frightened Mom, and she hurried to the telephone to call Grace Fung [her close friend].
>
> "What is this?" she asked. "Children in make-believe clothes at my front door!"

But soon, like many other immigrants, Fong-Torres's mother was dressing her children up to go trick-or-treating, only weeks after she served them moon cakes for the Harvest Moon Festival.

Text-Dependent Questions

1. Which color is considered especially lucky in traditional Chinese culture?
2. On which Chinese holiday do people honor their ancestors by cleaning gravesites and leaving offerings there?
3. Which traditional Chinese holiday features "moon cakes"?

Research Project

If you are of Chinese heritage, write about how your family celebrates a traditional holiday or festival, or about a specific celebration that was particularly memorable for you. If you aren't of Chinese heritage, research a traditional Chinese holiday or festival (such as the Chinese New Year, the Qingming Festival, the Dragon Boat Festival, or the Mid-Autumn Festival) and write a one-page report.

6 Tongs and Troubles

Any immigrants trying to make their way in an established ethnic enclave, and beyond that a larger, more integrated community, will face some difficulties. Recent Chinese immigrants are no exception. Their problems run across a wide spectrum, including labor exploitation, threats from tongs, language barriers in receiving medical and social services, and discrimination. Many of these problems are exacerbated by the large number of undocumented immigrants who come from China to the United States every year.

Illegal Immigration from China

It's impossible to say precisely how many Chinese undocumented immigrants are currently in the United States. A study by the Pew Research Center estimated that the number was about 300,000 in 2012. That would rank China as the fourth-largest source country for illegal immigrants to the United States. And there is broad consensus that illegal immigration from China is on the rise.

Some undocumented Chinese enter the country as virtual indentured servants for the people who smuggled them. Other newcomers have more mobility, but they still try to remain anonymous by not seeking government-funded medical services

◀ Marine police officers in the town of Aberdeen, Hong Kong, apprehend men trying to immigrate illegally. A complex network of smugglers helps Chinese immigrants arrive in North America through routes that are often circuitous.

or help from government or charitable organizations. Although they live in fear of being discovered and ultimately deported, many eventually find success by blending into the community, finding work and living a normal life without catching anyone's notice.

In June 1993, a ship filled with undocumented Chinese immigrants ran aground off the coast of the Queens borough of New York City. The *Golden Venture* carried almost 300 refugees, who for six months had nearly circled the globe in their small, rusty ship. At least 10 of the refugees died trying to swim to shore, while another 6 escaped into the United States undetected.

Eventually many of the refugees were deported back to China. In the following years, others who remained were granted political asylum. The *Golden Venture* incident brought the wretched conditions experienced by undocumented immigrants to the attention of the American media and fueled a public debate about refugees, political asylum, and human rights. Several similar incidents in which smugglers' boats have run aground along the coast of British Columbia have also taken place.

In recent years, according to U.S. and Canadian authorities, undocumented immigrants from China have increasingly been smuggled aboard fishing boats and in cargo ships, sealed in containers along with shipments of Chinese-manufactured products. Some would-be migrants don't survive the weeks-long journey

Words to Understand in This Chapter

indentured servant—a person who is obligated to work for another person (often without pay) in order to repay the costs of the journey to a new country.
refugee—a person who has been forced to leave his or country in order to escape war, persecution, or natural disaster.
triad—a secret society originating in China that is usually involved in organized crime.

US Coast Guard, FBI, and immigration officers move into position to open a cargo container suspected of housing Chinese migrants smuggled into the United States as dock workers place it on rolling supports. The container was aboard the motor vessel *Manoa* en route Los Angeles when crewmembers reported hearing tapping eminating from the container.

locked in a cargo container.

More affluent Chinese who want to settle in the United States or Canada but lack the proper authorization have a much safer and more comfortable alternative. They simply arrive as tourists and remain after their visas have expired.

Snakeheads

Chinese smugglers of undocumented immigrants are often referred to as "snakeheads," since the often circuitous route of the smuggling operation to North America resembles a snakes twisting body. The "little snakeheads" get the Chinese immigrants out of China safely, sometimes by legal means but more often illegally. The "big snakeheads" bring the undocumented immigrants into the United States or Canada.

An undocumented immigrant typically perceives the big snakeheads to be businesspeople instead of criminals. After all, the snakeheads are providing a needed service to Chinese immigrants, so it seldom concerns the undocumented immigrant that the smugglers are breaking U.S. or Canadian law.

Big snakeheads and their human cargo enter the country through a variety of routes and means of transportation. According to U.S. immigration authorities, one increasingly common (though still relatively rare) route involves a flight from China to Europe, another flight to South America, and a third flight to Mexico City. From there, the undocumented immigrants travel by land to northern Mexico, where they join undocumented Mexican immigrants crossing the U.S.–Mexican border, usually in areas where human-smuggling operations are already well established. Once they reach the border, the immigrants will often have to wait several days or even weeks in a Mexican "safe house." When their guides decide it is safe to attempt a crossing, they are brought into the United States and transported to their final destination.

Some immigrants also cross over, rather more easily, from Canada to the United States, or vice versa. In his book *Human Smuggling*, Kenneth Yates describes how immigrants from Fujian Province would fly into Canadian cities, then ask for political asylum in Canada or continue into the United States. Yates explains:

> Most aliens arriving [in Canada] from Fujian Province arrive at the Vancouver, Toronto, and Montreal airports.
>
> Current evidence indicates that a number of refugee claimants are delaying their entry into the customs inspection areas by hiding in bathroom facilities for several hours so investigators cannot ascertain which flight they arrived on. This is obviously an orchestrated ploy by the smuggling organizations to have the migrant evade detection.
>
> Once the aliens have been discovered in bathroom facilities, or after they enter the customs inspection area, they will immediately claim political asylum.

The air route is by far the most comfortable, consistent, and safest for immigrants coming illegally from China. It is, however, more expensive than the other routes and usually requires a forged passport and other documentation.

While it is cheaper, the sea route can be brutal for the undoc-

A Coast Guard cutter comes alongside a Chinese vessel at Midway Island. When the Coast Guard boarded the ship, they found more than 75 undocumented migrants aboard the freighter.

umented immigrant. A 19-year-old who was smuggled to the United States from Changle, in Fujian Province, told the story of her sea passage to researcher Ko-Lin Chin:

> We spent fifty-nine days on the mother ship. During those days, we ate twice daily. There was no water to wash ourselves, so we used seawater to brush our teeth and bathe. When we boarded the ship, every passenger was offered a thick paperboard and that was our bed. . . . When we were hungry, we tightened our belts. We did not even have the luxury to fill our stomachs with water when hungry. Many of us were seasick and could not eat much. Most of us lost a lot of weight, and we did not look like human beings.

Some passengers on the journey were denied water, developed skin diseases, or were assaulted by crew members.

Despite the hardships they may have endured in making their way to North America, some smuggled immigrants later become involved in the smuggling business themselves. For example, entrepreneurs from China's Fujian Province have been known to form organizations, called *shetous*, whose members meet migrants at the point of entry, collect travel documents, and take the newcomers to safe houses. The undocumented immigrants are forced to remain in these facilities until they have fully paid for the smuggling operation. Smuggling fees can cost up to $50,000, of which the *shetou* receives 10 percent. *Shetous* are also responsible for processing applications and hiring attorneys to help immigrants who are caught.

Paying Debts

Many undocumented Chinese immigrants can find work with Chinese employers, a fact that continues to draw immigrants to North America each year. Chinese owners of restaurants often hire people from their own hometowns, and some arrive without proper documents. In the United States, undocumented Chinese immigrants can apply for political asylum and are then allowed to work until their case is heard.

Smugglers may keep undocumented immigrants captive until their families or friends pay the smuggling fee. In some cases, the immigrants are kept in safe houses that are fairly sanitary, and they are provided with comfortable living conditions. But often residents are crowded into poorly heated, ramshackle dwellings or basements, where they receive substandard food and endure abominable conditions.

Those not held in safe houses must still pay off their debts. Sometimes they may be kidnapped and tortured, and relatives and friends who guaranteed payment may be threatened as well. In other cases undocumented immigrants are forced to pay off their debts by working for the smugglers or their associated gangs, sometimes as drug couriers, enforcers, or prostitutes. Because they arrived in the country without legal documentation and fear deportation, they usually do not contact the police or other government authorities when mistreated or forced into jobs they don't want.

Tongs, Triads, and Gangs

Some of the smuggling of drugs and humans occurs through Chinese organized crime syndicates that have been reported to operate through tongs and triads (secret Chinese societies usually consisting of related members). Some American government officials have claimed that a large share of money made from smuggling Chinese people goes directly into the tongs' pockets. In *Smuggled Chinese*, Ko-Lin Chin disagrees: "No doubt members of triads, tongs, and gangs are, to a certain extent, involved in trafficking Chinese, but I believe that their participation is neither sanctioned by nor even known to their respective organizations."

Most tongs are known to be involved in other criminal activities. These activities can entail the intimidation of those living in a tong-controlled territory of Chinatown. Tong members take money from local businesspeople with the understanding that the association will keep other tongs from threatening the business. Some Chinese refer to this kind of extortion as "lucky money"—it makes sure that the tong doesn't do anything

Chinese American teenagers who are prone to commit illegal activity may join gangs. These gangs, some of which have connections with the larger tong organizations of Chinatown neighborhoods, falsely promise power and influence to those youths who may lack employment and educational opportunities.

"unlucky" to the business, like smashing its windows or stealing its shipments of goods.

Some Chinese youth involved in criminal activity belong to Chinatown gangs, which may have tong connections. In New York City's Chinatown a tong-affiliated youth gang often enforces the tong's dictates on the streets. Some researchers have observed that immigrant teens may be drawn to gangs and later to tongs because through these groups they acquire power and influence in the community and are given important responsibilities. Others claim that many Chinatown gangs using the name *tong* actually have no connections to the larger associations. Instead the youth gangs are simply comprised of uneducated young immigrants dissatisfied with the lack of employment and economic opportunities.

In her book *Chinatown*, Gwen Kinkead quotes David Chen, executive director of the Chinese-American Planning Council, who sheds some light on how problems for Chinese youth have led to gang problems in some Chinatown neighborhoods. According to Chen,

> Many adults are illiterate in Chinatown. So the kids run the households. It contradicts the Chinese way of life, which is to respect the elders. It leads to a lot of problems: the kids hang out, there's not enough housing; there's not enough parental guidance; and at the same time, there's too much pressure for performance in school. They're all supposed to be stereotypical whiz kids. And those who aren't end up in gangs.

Racial Discrimination and Poverty

The Chinese in North America have endured a long history of discrimination. The 1882 Chinese Exclusion Act, which remained in place for 60 years, prevented immigration and naturalization on the basis of race. For decades the Chinese already living in the United States faced many obstacles: they were excluded from the right to obtain citizenship, vote, own land, or place their children in regular public schools.

The traditional Chinatowns used to offer a haven from physical danger for their inhabitants. Before the Second World War,

Chinese children who ventured outside Chinatown in San Francisco, New York, or Los Angeles were frequently pelted with stones and garbage by white children. English-speaking natives would mock the Chinese language by making nonsense sounds. While the Chinese today generally face far less bigotry, it is still possible for ethnic tensions to develop.

Employment concerns often affect how native residents feel toward new immigrants. When large numbers of foreigners settle in a neighborhood, its U.S.–born residents may worry that their jobs will be taken by the newcomers. However, economic studies have shown this generally doesn't happen. New immigrants not only benefit from coming to America, but their contributions to the economy also benefit their neighbors.

The conditions found in Chinatowns during the 1960s reveal the extreme hardship and poverty endured by many Chinese who immigrated in those years. In his book *The Rice Room*, Ben Fong-Torres described the living environment typical of New York City's Chinatown at the time:

This cartoon from 1882 shows American immigrant workers building a wall to keep out Chinese immigrants. That year the US Congress passed the Chinese Exclusion Act.

Tongs and Troubles   93

An American eats at a Chinese restaurant with his newly adopted Chinese daughter. As a result of China's one-child policy, many Chinese families favor having sons, who will remain a permanent part of the family, and decide to put up their daughters for adoption.

Families of six to eight shared single hotel rooms, with a plank of plywood over a bathtub serving as a dining table. Clothes were stored in old trunks or stuffed into shopping bags hung on nails. Older single men slept in tiered bunkbeds in dank, closet-sized rooms.

During the 1960s many newcomers and residents suffered from malnutrition, lack of exercise, and tuberculosis. Similar problems existed in San Francisco's inner-city Chinatown. A 1970s study by researcher Ling-chi Wang recorded substandard housing in two-thirds of the living quarters, and tuberculosis rates that were six times the national average. However, conditions in these Chinese enclaves have improved markedly for immigrants, as the awareness of public health issues has grown.

China's Adopted Daughters

The Chinese government's implementation of the one-child policy had a significant effect on Chinese immigration. It impelled many Chinese citizens who wanted to have more children to leave the country, and it also left many orphan girls available to be adopted by American parents. This second consequence is the result of the traditional preference for males in Chinese culture:

sons remain a part of the family even after marriage, while daughters join their husbands' families.

Many American couples have adopted Chinese girls who were abandoned by their parents in China. Since they are brought over from China as babies, most have no recollection of their mothers' or caregivers' faces or of the Chinese language or culture. Although some adoptive parents are Chinese, people of all ethnicities have also chosen to adopt Chinese girls. Non-Chinese adoptive families often face many decisions, including how to provide their daughters with information about the Chinese and Chinese American cultures and how to help them deal with prejudice or other issues they potentially face growing up in a different culture.

Text-Dependent Questions

1. What was the *Golden Venture*?
2. What is a "snakehead"?
3. Identify some of the dangers faced by Chinese undocumented immigrants.

Research Project

To become a U.S. citizen, an immigrant from another country must pass a civics test. U.S. Citizenship and Immigration Services offers practice tests at: https://my.uscis.gov/prep/test/civics/view

Take a test. What percentage did you get correct? Do some further research about any answers you got wrong.

7 Part of the Mosaic, Part of the Melting Pot

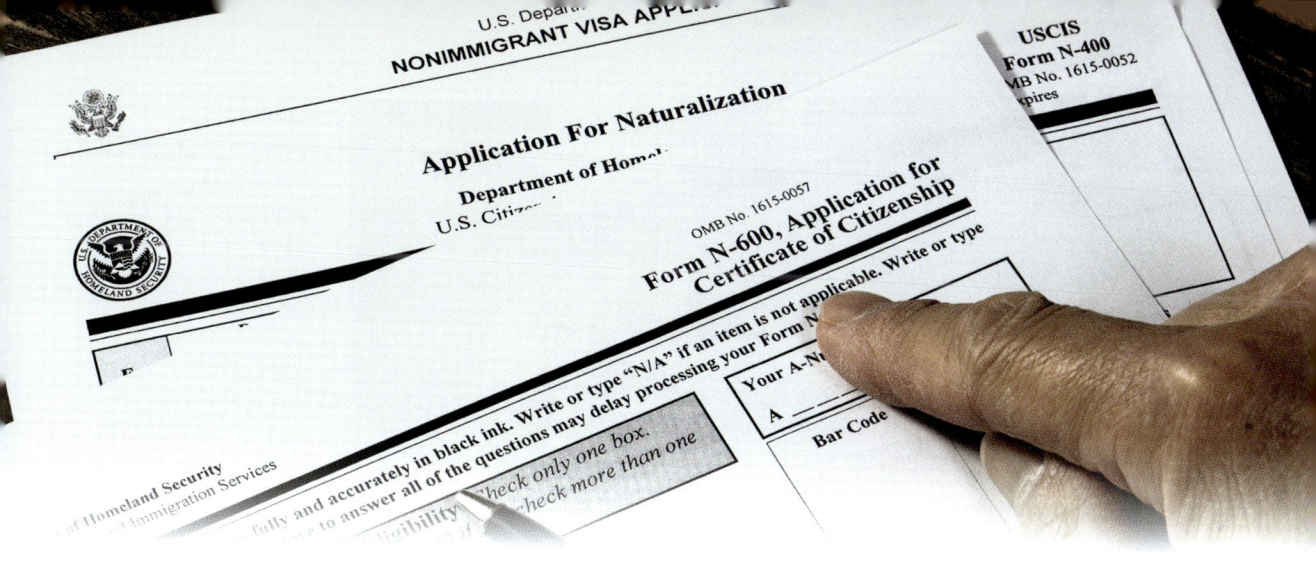

In 2010, according to the U.S. census, Americans of full or partial Chinese ancestry made up about 1.3 percent of the country's overall population. Official Canadian figures, meanwhile, show that ethnic Chinese accounted for 4 percent of Canada's population in 2011. In both countries, Chinese constituted the largest Asian group.

A Growing Population

In the years ahead, the Chinese will no doubt have a major impact on the face of North America. China ranks among the top source countries for immigrants to the United States and to Canada. Between 2000 and 2013, the United States admitted nearly 890,000 legal immigrants from mainland China, in addition to 185,000 from Hong Kong and Taiwan. From 2006 to 2011, Canada admitted more than 120,000 Chinese immigrants.

It is likely that the high rate of immigration from China to North America will continue. Although economic conditions in China have improved greatly in recent decades, the standard of living and high wages available in North America continue to attract tens of thousands of Chinese each year.

◀ The diverse populace of the United States is sometimes likened to a cultural mosaic, of which Chinese Americans—the largest Asian American group at an estimated 4.1 million people—make up a significant piece.

A Chinese American man sits in New York's Columbus Park reading a Chinese-language newspaper.

In the years ahead, immigration researchers will probably have difficulty charting the exact numbers of Chinese immigrants illegally entering North America; however, some analysts believe that the steady flow of this immigrant group is unlikely to abate.

Making Significant Contributions

The influence of Chinese immigrants—both legal and undocumented—on Western society is apparent in the growing

Words to Understand in This Chapter

AIDS—acquired immunodeficiency syndrome, a disease of the human immune system.
calligraphy—stylized or elegant lettering, practiced as an art form in China.
qigong—an ancient Chinese healing art involving meditation, controlled breathing, and movement exercises (pronounced chee-gung).

Performers participate in a dragon dance during the Chinese New Year celebration in San Francisco. Traditions preserved by Chinese Americans have made a significant impact on mainstream North American culture.

A Future of Possibilities

Ellis Island of the West

During the early 20th century, Chinese immigrants docking at San Francisco were quickly shuttled onto ferries that carried them to an immigration station located in the middle of the bay on Angel Island. From 1910 to 1940, this site was commonly referred to as the "Ellis Island of the West." Approximately one million immigrants, mostly from Asia, were processed at the facility.

But unlike Ellis Island, where most new immigrants usually waited a few hours for processing, Angel Island kept immigrants waiting for at least two weeks, and even as long as two years. They were housed in rough wooden barracks, kept under guard, and allowed out only for meals and to exercise in an area enclosed by a 12-foot-high barbed-wire fence.

The Chinese were kept in the Angel Island barracks for the longest period out of all the immigrant groups, because under the Chinese Exclusion Act of 1882 they were not allowed to enter the United States unless they were wives and children of American citizens or were entering as merchants, students, diplomats, or tourists. Before being approved to enter the United States, they were closely interrogated to determine their eligibility.

In 1970 a park ranger discovered Chinese calligraphy that had been carved into the walls of the barracks. It was in the form of poems written by immigrants living in the barracks. Eventually more than 100 poems were uncovered, most of them reflecting the fear and sadness felt by the Chinese forced to linger there. They were documented by researchers as part of an eight-year, $32-million project to restore Angel Island and tell the story of its role in early Asian immigration.

---

popularity of many aspects of their culture, particularly Chinese food, martial arts, and medicine. People of all ages and ethnic backgrounds practice the Chinese martial arts of tai chi and kung fu, and ancient Chinese healing practices such as acupuncture and *qigong* have found a place in Western mainstream medicine.

Although they were prevented during the first half of the 20th century from obtaining citizenship and participating in political systems, Chinese Americans had begun making their presence known in politics and government by the 1970s. Through advocacy groups, they have worked to obtain and protect their rights in the United States and Canada. Today they serve in courtrooms, in city council chambers, and in local, state, and federal government.

Many Chinese Americans have been responsible for contributions in technology and science. They have helped design defense systems, silicon chips, computer software, and the Internet. Scientific researchers have received Nobel prizes for discoveries in chemistry and physics, and have developed treatments for deadly illnesses such as AIDS. Those living 100 or even 50 years ago could hardly have predicted the great impact that Chinese immigrants would make on American and Canadian life.

Text-Dependent Questions

1. Which country has a greater percentage of ethnic Chinese residents, the United States or Canada?
2. Where is Angel Island? What role did it play in Chinese immigration to the United States?
3. Since 2000, has the United States admitted more immigrants from mainland China or from Taiwan and Hong Kong combined?

Research Project

Choose a famous Chinese American or Chinese Canadian and write a short profile of that person.

Famous Central Americans

JACKIE CHAN (1954–), Hollywood star, one of the few actors to perform all his own stunts; his action/comedy hit films include *Rumble in the Bronx* (1996), *Rush Hour* (1998), *Shanghai Noon* (2000), *Shanghai Knights* (2003), *Rush Hour 2* (2001), *Rush Hour 3* (2007), and *Dragon Blade* (2015).

DAVID HO (1952–), chemist and director of the Aaron Diamond AIDS Research Center; his groundbreaking research work on protease inhibitors, which reduce the level of HIV, has helped allow AIDS patients to live longer after diagnosis.

JI-LI JIANG (1954–), children's book author; a former science teacher and founder of her own business, East West Exchange, she is the author of the award-winning novel *Red Scarf Girl* (1997), which is based on memories of her teenage years in Communist China. Her second book, *Magical Monkey King—Mischief in Heaven* (2002), is based on a Chinese folk tale.

ANG LEE (1954–), art-film director of *Sense and Sensibility* (1995), *Ride with the Devil* (1999), and *Crouching Tiger, Hidden Dragon* (2000), which won an Oscar for best foreign language film. Lee also directed *The Hulk* (2003), the blockbuster based on the comic-book hero. Lee has won the Academy Award for Best Director twice: for *Brokeback Mountain* (2005) and for *Life of Pi* (2012).

YUAN T. LEE (1936–), chemist and recipient of the Nobel Prize in Chemistry in 1986 for his discoveries concerning the dynamics of elementary chemical processes; he was also awarded the National Medal of Science in 1986.

JEREMY LIN (1988–), a professional basketball player who has starred for several NBA teams, is the U.S.-born son of immigrants from Taiwan.

LUCY LIU (1968–), actress whose film credits include Kung Fu Panda, Kill Bill: Vol. 1, and Kill Bill: Vol. 2 and whose television work includes the popular series Elementary.

BILL MOW (1937–), founder, chairman, and CEO of Bugle Boy Industries, a casual-wear clothing line; he also holds a Ph.D. in electrical engineering.

I. M. PEI (1917–), architect, designer of modern skyscrapers, housing projects, museums, and academic and government buildings; for his designs he has received a multitude of awards, including the Medal of Freedom, Medal of Liberty, Grande Medaille d'Or, and Japanese Praemium Imperiale.

Vivienne Tam (1975–), fashion designer and founder of high fashion boutiques; in her book China Chic, published in 2000, she chronicled the history of Chinese dress and culture.

An Wang (1920–1990), founder of Wang Laboratories, a company that develops specialty electronic devices; his contributions to the development of digital computing machines helped revolutionize the information-processing industry.

Wayne Wang (1949–), film director whose movies often deal with issues related to China and Chinese Americans; his most successful films include *The Joy Luck Club* (1993) and *Chinese Box* (1997), which is set before and during the transfer of Hong Kong from British to Chinese possession.

Harry Hongda Wu (1937–), geologist, writer, and activist; in 1985, after spending 19 years in a Chinese prison, he immigrated to the United States, where he became an advocate for democracy and human rights in China.

Series Glossary of Key Terms

assimilate—to adopt the ways of another culture; to fully become part of a different country or society.

census—an official count of a country's population.

deport—to forcibly remove someone from a country, usually back to his or her native land.

green card—a document that denotes lawful permanent resident status in the United States.

migrant laborer—an agricultural worker who travels from region to region, taking on short-term jobs.

naturalization—the act of granting a foreign-born person citizenship.

passport—a paper or book that identifies the holder as the citizen of a country; usually required for traveling to or through other foreign lands.

undocumented immigrant—a person who enters a country without official authorization; sometimes referred to as an "illegal immigrant."

visa—official authorization that permits arrival at a port of entry but does not guarantee admission into the United States.

Further Reading

Boli, Zhang. *Escape from China: The Long Journey from Tiananmen to Freedom*. New York: Washington Square Press, 2002.

Chin, Ko-Lin. *Smuggled Chinese: Clandestine Immigration to the United States*. Philadelphia: Temple University Press, 1999.

Evans, Karin. *The Lost Daughters of China*. New York: Tarcher/Putnam, 2000.

Fallows, James. *China Airborne: The Test of China's Future*. New York: Vintage Books, 2013.

Lee, Erika. *The Making of Asian America*. New York: Simon and Schuster, 2015.

Merino, Noel. *Illegal Immigration*. San Diego: Greenhaven Press, 2015.

Osnos, Evan. *Age of Ambition: Chasing Fortune, Truth, and Faith in the New China*. New York: Farrar, Straus & Giroux, 2014.

Takaki, Ronald. *Strangers from a Different Shore: A History of Asian Americans*. Boston: Back Bay Books, 1998.

Wu, Harry Hongda, and Carolyn Wakeman. *Bitter Winds: A Memoir of My Years in China's Gulag*. New York: John Wiley and Sons, 1994.

Internet Resources

www.c-c-c.org
The Chinese Cultural Center of San Francisco has information about visiting hours, exhibits, and Chinese cultural events.

www.capa-news.org
CAPA News is the main website for the Chinese American Political Association.

www.goldsea.com
Gold Sea Asian American Daily includes news, feature stories, opinion pieces, and more.

www.ocanatl.org
The national website of OCA–Asian Pacific American Advocates provides event listings, news, and activism information.

www.wn.com/s/chineseamericanews
Chinese America News provides information on political and social issues pertaining to Chinese Americans.

www.cia.gov/library/publications/the-world-factbook/geos/ch.html
The CIA World Factbook's China page.

Publisher's Note: The websites listed on this page were active at the time of publication. The publisher is not responsible for websites that have changed their address or discontinued operation since the date of publication. The publisher reviews and updates the websites each time the book is reprinted.

Index

1882 Chinese Exclusion Act. *See* Chinese Exclusion Act of 1882
1976 Immigration Act (Canada), 52
1952 Immigration and Nationality Act, 42–43
1965 Immigration and Nationality Act, **42**, 43, 47, 49

acupuncture, 17, 96
    See also culture
American Association of Commerce and Industry, 68
Angel Island, **39**, 94
Asian American Experiences in the United States (Lee), 26–27, 73, 75
Autumn Moon Festival, 79
    See also holidays

Bitter Winds (Wu), 41
Boli, Zhang, 32
Boston, Mass., 60
Buddhism, 25, 37
    See also religion
Bureau of Citizenship and Immigration Services (BCIS), 45
Bureau of Customs and Border Protection (BCBP), 45
Bureau of Immigration and Customs Enforcement (BICE), 45
Bush, George H. W., 55
Bush, George W., **34**, **45**

Canada
    Chinese population in, 19, 93, **96**
    immigration history, 18–19, 51–55
    immigration rates, 18–19, 93
Canadian Citizenship Act of 1947, 54
Carter, Jimmy, **30**
Chan, Anthony, 54
Chan, Jackie, **80**, 98
Chan Kong-Sang. *See* Chan, Jackie

Chen, David, 88
Chiang Kai-Shek, 21–22
    See also Nationalist Party
Chicago, Ill., 60
Chin, Ko-Lin, 63, 85, 87
Chin, Vincent, 61
    See also discrimination
China
    economy, 23–24, 35, 63, 93–94
    ethnic groups in, 16–17
    history, 21–35
    and Hong Kong, 34–35
    population, 15–16, 29, 35
    religion, 17–18
    and the United States, 26, **30**, 49, 54–55, 76
China Men (Kingston), 76
Chinatown (Kinkead), 65, 88
Chinatowns, 15, **57**, 58–60, 64–65, 78, 81, 89, 90
    gangs in, 87–88
        See also communities
Chinese-American Planning Council, 67, 88
Chinese Americans
    communities, 57–60
    discrimination against, 48, 60, 61, **62**, 65, 88–90, **94**
    education, 64
    employment, 50, 60–65, 86
    family structure, 65–67, 74–76, 88, 90–91
    immigration rates of, **16**, 18–19, 48–49, 93
    population, 19, **58**, 59, 93
    See also culture
Chinese Benevolent Association of Canada, 54
Chinese Canadian National Council (CCNC), 69, 71
Chinese Consolidated Benevolent Association (CCBA), 67–68, 69

Numbers in ***bold italic*** refer to captions.

Chinese Culture Foundation, 71
Chinese Exclusion Act of 1882, 39–40, 88, **89**, 94
    See also quotas
Chinese Historical Society of America, 71
Chinese New Year, **73**, **75**, 76–79, 80, **95**
    See also holidays
Chinese Student Adjustment Act of 1992, 55
Chinese Zodiac, 77
    See also culture
Communist Party, 21–26, 28–31, 34–35, 54–55
    and the Tiananmen Square Democracy Movement, 32–34
    See also China
communities, 57–60
    See also Chinatowns
Cultural Revolution, **22**, 24–26, **27**, 28, 37
    See also Communist Party
culture, 65–66, 69, 71, 73–81, 95–97
    See also Chinese Americans; family structure

Deng Xiaoping, 25, **27**, 28–29, **30**, 34, 36
    See also Communist Party
Department of Homeland Security, 44–45
Detroit, Mich., 61
discrimination, 48, 60, 61, **62**, 65, 88–90, 94
Displaced Persons Act of 1948, 42
    See also refugees

economy
    China, 23–24, 35, 63, 93–94
    United States, 63
employment, 50, 60–65, 86
Enhanced Border Security and Visa Entry Reform Act (2002), 44, **45**
Escape from China (Boli), **32**
ethnicity, 16–17, 39, 61
    See also quotas

Falun Gong, **36**, 37
    See also religion
family structure, 65–67, 74–76, 88, 90–91
    See also culture
Fermi, Laura, 41
Fong-Torres, Ben, 74, 81, 90
Four Brothers Association, 68
"Four Modernizations," 28
    See also Deng Xiaoping
Fukien American Association, 68

Gang of Four, 26, **27**, 28
    See also Mao Zedong
gangs. *See* tongs
Gold Mountain (Chan), 54
Golden Venture, 83–84
    See also undocumented immigrants
Grant, Madison, 40

Haifeng, Guo, 32
hate crimes. *See* discrimination
Ho, David, 98
holidays, **73**, **75**, 76–81
    See also culture
Homeland Security Act of 2002, 44–45
    See also Department of Homeland Security
Hong Kong, 16, 25, 34–36, 49, 54
    See also China
Hood, Marlowe, 63
Houston, Tex., 60
Hua Guofeng, 28
    See also Communist Party
human rights, 25, **31**, 32, 37, 41, 47, 55
Human Smuggling (Yates), 85

illegal immigrants. *See* undocumented immigrants
Illegal Immigration Reform and Immigrant Responsibility Act (1996), 44
immigration
    difficulties of, 83
    history of, in Canada, 18–19, 51–55
    history of, in the United States, 39–49, 54–55
    rates of, in Canada, 18–19, 93
    rates of, in the United States, **16**, 18–19, 41–42, 46, 48–49, 93
    reasons for, 26–27, 31, 34, 35, 37, 39, 63–64, 90, 93–94
Immigration Act of 1924, 40–41
Immigration Act of 1990, 44
Immigration Act of 1952 (Canada), 51–52
Immigration and Nationality Act of 1952, 42–43
Immigration and Nationality Act of 1965, **42**, 43, 47, 49
Immigration and Naturalization Service (INS), 43–44, 45–46
    See also Department of Homeland Security
Immigration and Refugee Protection Act (Canada), 52–53

Immigration Reform and Control Act (1986), 44

Japan, 21, 48–49
Jiang, Ji-li, 98
Jiang Qing, 26, **27**
Jiang Zemin, 34–35
Johnson, Lyndon B., **42**

Kai-Shek, Chiang. *See* Chiang Kai-Shek
Kingston, Maxine Hong, 76
Kinkead, Gwen, 65, 88
Kuhn, Robert Lawrence, 35

Lai, Kenny, 26–27
languages, 17, 59
Lantern Festival, **78**, 79
   See also holidays
Laughlin, Harry N., 40
Lee, Ang, 98
Lee, Bruce, 80
Lee, Joann Faung Jean, 26–27, 73
Lee, Yuan T., 98
"Little Red Book," **22**, 23
   See also Mao Zedong
Liu, Jeng, 63–64
Loo, Ming Hai "Jim," 61
   See also discrimination
Los Angeles, Calif., 57
lunar calendar, 77
   See also culture
Macao, 16
   See also China
Made in China (Kuhn), 35
Mao Zedong, 21–26, 27–28, **29**, 41
   See also Communist Party
Meng, Bai, 32
Mid-Autumn Festival. *See* Autumn Moon Festival
Mow, Bill, 98

National Asian Pacific American Legal Consortium (NAPALC), 90
Nationalist Party, 21–22, 54–55, 68, 81
   See also China
New York City, N.Y., 59, 69
Nixon, Richard, 26, **30**

one-child policy, 29–30, 90–91
   See also Communist Party
Organization of Chinese Americans, 71, 77
organizations, 54, 67–71

Pearson, Lester, 52
Pei, I. M., 98
People's Republic of China. *See* China
Philadelphia, Penn., **57**, 60
points system, 52
   See also Canada
population
   China, 15–16, 29, 35
   Chinese, in Canada, 19, 93, **96**
   Chinese Americans, 19, **58**, 59, 93

Qing Ming, 79
   See also holidays
quotas, 40–42, 43, 49, 53
   See also immigration
Quotations from Chairman Mao Zedong ("Little Red Book"), **22**, 23

Red Guards, 24–26
   See also Communist Party
Refugee Act of 1980, 44
refugees, 42, 44, 48, 51, 84
religion, 17–18, 25, 37, 67, **70**
   See also Falun Gong
The Rice Room (Fong-Torres), 74, 90

Sakamoto, Arthur, 63–64
San Francisco, Calif., 57, 60, 65, 90
Scully, C. D., 40
Seattle, Wash., 57
She, Colleen, 66
shetous, 86
   See also undocumented immigrants
Six Companies, 67
Smuggled Chinese (Chin), 63, 87
snakeheads, 84
   See also undocumented immigrants
Spring Festival. *See* Chinese New Year
Strangers from a Different Shore (Takaki), 48
Suettinger, Sue Jean Lee, 75–76
Sung, Betty Lee, 74

Taiwan, 15–16, 22, 36, 55, 68, 69, 81
   See also China
Takaki, Ronald, 48, 49
Tam, Vivienne, 98
Teenage Refugees from China Speak Out (She), 66
Temporary Quota Act of 1921, 40
Tiananmen Square Democracy Movement, 32–34, 55
   See also Communist Party

Tibet, 16, 25, 37
   See also China
tongs, 68–69, 87–88
   See also organizations
tongxianghui, 68
   See also organizations
Toronto, Ontario, **57**, 60
triads, 87
   See also tongs

undocumented immigrants, 19, 44, 45, 46, 83–87, 94
United Chinese Associations of New York, 68
United Fujianese of American Association, 68
United States
   and China, 26, **30**, 49, 54–55, 76
   Chinese American population in, 15, **58**, 59, 93
   economy, 63
   immigration history, 39–49, 54–55
   immigration rates, **16**, 18–19, 41–42, 46, 48–49, 93
USA PATRIOT Act (2002), 44, **45**

Vancouver, British Columbia, 57, **59**, 60
visas, 40, 44, 47
   See also immigration

Wang, An, 98
Wang, Ling-chi, 90
Wang, Wayne, 99
Wang Hongwen, 26
The Wasp, **89**
World War I, 40
World War II, 21–22, 40, 42, 48–49, 51, 53
Wu, Harry Hongda, 41, 99

Xiaoping, Deng. See Deng Xiaoping

Yao Wenyuan, 26
Yates, Kenneth, 85
Yuan, Chen, 63

Zedong, Mao. See Mao Zedong
Zhang Chunqiao, 26
Zhou Enlai, 28

Contributors

Senior consulting editor STUART ANDERSON is an adjunct scholar at the Cato Institute and executive director of the National Foundation for American Policy. From August 2001 to January 2003, he served as executive associate commissioner for Policy and Planning and Counselor to the Commissioner at the Immigration and Naturalization Service. He spent four and a half years on Capitol Hill on the Senate Immigration Subcommittee, first for Senator Spencer Abraham and then as Staff Director of the subcommittee for Senator Sam Brownback. Prior to that, Stuart was Director of Trade and Immigration Studies at the Cato Institute, where he produced reports on the military contributions of immigrants and the role of immigrants in high technology. Stuart has published articles in the Wall Street Journal, New York Times, Los Angeles Times, and other publications. He has an M.A. from Georgetown University and a B.A. in Political Science from Drew University. His articles have appeared in such publications as the *Wall Street Journal*, *New York Times*, and *Los Angeles Times*.

MARIAN L. SMITH served as the senior historian of the U.S. Immigration and Naturalization Service (INS) from 1988 to 2003, and is currently the immigration and naturalization historian within the Department of Homeland Security in Washington, D.C. She studies, publishes, and speaks on the history of the immigration agency and is active in the management of official 20th-century immigration records.

PETER HAMMERSCHMIDT is director general of national cyber security at Public Safety Canada. He previously served as First Secretary (Financial and Military Affairs) for the Permanent Mission of Canada to the United Nations. Before taking this position, he was a ministerial speechwriter and policy specialist for the Department of National Defence in Ottawa. Prior to joining the public service, he served as the Publications Director for the Canadian Institute of Strategic Studies in Toronto. He has a B.A. (Honours) in Political Studies from Queen's University, and an MScEcon in Strategic Studies from the University of Wales, Aberystwyth.

JIAO GAN is a freelance writer and editor. He was born in Beijing, and came to the United States in 1987. He lives in New York City with his wife and two children. This is his first book.

Picture Credits

Page
- 1: Rightdx / Shutterstock.com
- 2: Kamira / Shutterstock.com
- 9: used under license from Shutterstock, Inc.
- 12: used under license from Shutterstock, Inc.
- 14: ChameleonsEye / Shutterstock.com
- 18: OTTN Publishing
- 20: Hulton/Archive/Getty Images
- 23: Everett Historical
- 24: Everett Historical
- 27: Everett Historical
- 32: Hulton/Archive/Getty Images
- 35: Bettmann/Corbis
- 36: courtesy Jimmy Carter Presidential Library
- 39: Kevin Lee/Newsmakers/Getty Images
- 41: Corbis Images
- 43: United Nations photo
- 44: Bartlomie Magierowski / Shutterstock.com
- 46: A. Katz / Shutterstock.com
- 48: Alexander Image / Shutterstock.com
- 52: courtesy Lyndon B. Johnson Presidential Library
- 53: Alex Wong/Getty Images
- 54: Chinese swaring in citizen
- 56: OTTN Publishing
- 57: OTTN Publishing
- 58: Chinahbzyg / Shutterstock.com
- 60: Mandritoiu / Shutterstock.com
- 63: 1000 Words / Shutterstock.com
- 65: f11photo / Shutterstock.com
- 66: Jorg Hackemann / Shutterstock.com
- 70: used under license from Shutterstock, Inc.
- 74: Sergei Bachlakov / Shutterstock.com
- 77: Kobby Dagan / Shutterstock.com
- 80: Featureflash Photo Agency / Shutterstock.com
- 82: Sean Pavone / Shutterstock.com
- 84: Donna Day/ImageState
- 87: US Coast Guard photo
- 89: US Coast Guard photo
- 91: 1000 Words / Shutterstock.com
- 93: Everett Historical
- 94: Peter Parks/AFP/Getty Images
- 96: used under license from Shutterstock, Inc.
- 98: Alexander Image / Shutterstock.com
- 99: used under license from Shutterstock, Inc.